DISAPPEARING OVERNIGHT

Ken Tracey

Grosvenor House
Publishing Limited

This book is published by
Grosvenor House Publishing Ltd
Link House
140 The Broadway, Tolworth, Surrey, KT6 7HT.
www.grosvenorhousepublishing.co.uk

This book is a work of fiction. Any resemblance to
people or events, past or present, is purely coincidental.

A CIP record for this book
is available from the British Library

ISBN 978-1-83975-236-0

Stories previously published;

Hat Trick; Copyright 2013 Ken Tracey.
Back in Tennessee; Copyright 2016 Ken Tracey.
Disappearing Over Night; Copyright 2017 Ken Tracey.

To

Tilly, Kyle, Jake, Mathew, Sam, Adam,
Liam and Daniel.

The Author

Ken Tracey writes short fiction with a sting in the tail. He is a chartered quantity surveyor, born in Liverpool, and has worked in Africa, Europe and around the UK. His interest in people and the astonishing situations that they create, inspire his stories. His Northern humour and contact with the wacky world of construction, combine to create interesting characters. He is the author of feature articles and memoir published in magazines and newspapers. He blogs on his website www.kentracey.co.uk A keen walker, who seldom passes a country pub, he lives in Kent with his wife and seven goldfish.

Contents

Disappearing Overnight

The man who despised capitalism chose to meet me in the Grosvenor Hotel, Victoria. A sign that he was unlike the other defectors I had helped and a sign that this night would be different. He was to carry out his day's business as usual, until he entered the lounge with his fiancé and joined me for a drink. Then his life would change forever.

It was dark outside and each bus that wheezed along Buckingham Palace Road displayed its top deck passengers slumped in a haze, with fags dangling from their mouths. I knew that they would achieve nothing, and never share in the wealth that they were crippling themselves to produce. Now it would get worse with petrol at fifty pence a gallon and the effects of inflation and strikes.

If only I could leave it all behind too and go with this Felix fellow tonight, to live in a fair society. Leave these pre-dinner drinkers in their double-breasted penguin suits and their maxi-skirted wives.

The waiter paused with a raised eyebrow, so I ordered another vodka. The grandfather clock and my Sekonda agreed that Felix was ten minutes late. I would have expected more accuracy from a scientist.

Two gulps of my fresh drink had gone and I'd taken to cracking my knuckles, when a gangerly young man walked in. 'I'm meeting someone;' I heard him answer the waiter's enquiry.

Immediately I discounted him as my contact. He was alone anyway, and wore a black overcoat that almost swept the floor. His hair was shoulder length beneath a black fedora and he squeaked along in those new training shoes. More like Mick Jagger than a scientist. But he kept coming, and next thing I was standing up and shaking his outstretched hand.

'Felix.' His mischievous grin revealed tombstone teeth.

'Alex,' I replied. He'd dispensed with the safety of code words. I told him to sit down.

He removed the coat with a flourish and draped it over a chair, where it did touch the floor. The fedora was cast on the table and he stretched back in an arm chair.

'Don't get comfortable, we have to leave soon.' Already this job was different.

'Sh.' He was about to speak and the waiter was at my shoulder. I ordered a whiskey.

'Thanks for that,' he chuckled. 'How did you know my tipple?'

'We know everything.' I lied; in fact, I'd smelt it on his breath. All I really knew was that he worked on some clever stuff that valued him highly with the Soviets, and I would deliver him and his fiancé to an address in Kensington Palace Gardens.

'Where is Sandra?'

He slid back a crumpled sleeve and studied a diver's watch. 'She should be here.'

'But she isn't. Where can she be?'

'She's coming after work, must have been delayed.'

'You should have brought her with you. Where does she work?' I was disappointed.

'It's only five minutes from here. She's a nanny in a family house.'

'OK, we'll finish our drinks and go get her.'

The lounge was filling up; sparkling glasses were being raised along with the volume of chatter. We would need to be discreet; Harold Wilson's election victory was enough for the elite to suspect reds everywhere.

'Sounds like an interesting job you have.' I knew that he'd be cautious about his work, but we needed to warm up.

'We've made progress,' he smirked.

Would I learn why the Soviets wanted this odd ball, or would I be left guessing?

'What's your specialty?' I tried again.

It took a wrinkled brow and several seconds for him to reduce his reply to my level. 'Basically, it's Physics. You'll know of Einstein and Planck?'

One out of two would have to do, I nodded.

'Well our work stems from their theories, but we've had a breakthrough with the transference of matter. That's why I must share my research for the benefit of the people.'

Admirable, but he'd lost me, 'transference of matter,' sounded really Sci-Fi. He drained his glass and glanced around the room. It was clearly a full stop to further explanation.

'We are going to collect Sandra now.' I pushed my glass away. 'While we're on the street you must be alert for danger. Watch me at all times and do as I say without question.'

'OK,' but the student of Planck hadn't convinced me.

With a grip on his arm, I steered my prize through the traffic jamming Buckingham Palace Road. He directed me into Belgravia where Sandra worked and fortunately where I had parked.

'When we have Sandra, we'll be travelling by car. I'm parked just past that pub on the right.' Ahead light splashed the pavement.

'The house is beyond the pub', he answered.

We quickened our pace, if Sandra wasn't there, I would have to cajole Felix into leaving without her. The procedure was to tell them that their loved ones would join them later, and sometimes they did.

The drone of beery conversation and the tang of cigarette smoke greeted us. Felix cupped his hands to his eyes to see through the pub window. I made for the shadows and waited at the steps of a neighbouring house.

When he caught up, the shoulders of the great coat shrugged. 'She might have gone in there by mistake.' I doubted that a physicist's fiancée would confuse The Plumbers Arms with the Grosvenor, but said, 'Let's try the house first.' We were losing momentum.

We passed my car sandwiched between a Mini and a Ford Corsair, lots of space, I could get out easily.

Suddenly, footsteps clattered ahead. I strained to see through the dark. A woman in a mini dress ran toward us.

'Felix, is this her?' I hissed.

'Can't tell yet.' We stopped a few feet apart.

'Help me,' she cried as she ran.' She didn't pass between us but dropped sobbing into Felix's arms. 'He's killed her.'

She was too close to my prize. I grabbed her wrist and pulled her to me. The tears on her face glistened in the street light. She was about my own age, thirty, skinny with long hair and her dress was stained with blood.

'Is this your friend?' I was sure she didn't match the picture I'd seen of Sandra.

'No. No but she's bleeding, Alex. We've got to help.'

'Get away from her. Look you've got blood on your coat now. Get in the car'

I held her wrist with one hand and threw him the keys with the other.

'Do you want the police?' My face was close to hers.

'He's killed her', she bleated.

'Who has?'

'My husband.'

A murder on the street would foul up my operation. 'Go to the pub. They'll call the police for you. Quick, quick.' I shoved her away and she scurried off.

'Hold on, Alex.' It was Felix

'Get in the fucking car. Now.' He scowled and shuffled away. 'What's the number of the house where Sandra works?'

'Forty-six,' he mumbled,

'Keep off the street until I get back.' I took off and didn't slow down until twin columns with the house number on came into view. Lights glowed on the upper floors. At the top of the steps I beat on the door and stood back. I noticed a man on the opposite side of the road his face toward me, he didn't stop. I hoped that a servant would open the door I didn't want to confront the family.

There was no answer. The woman would cause a stir at the pub and they would be quick to call the police and the response to this prestigious address would be pretty damn quick. The thought of the street sealed off and blue lights slicing the night made me beat the door with both fists.

Nothing and it was 10 pm already. There was a dim light on in the basement. Back at street level, I pushed open an iron gate to the basement area, then clattered down the steps. An open door brought me to a halt. Surely this was where the staff would be. I'd give Sandra just two minutes to leave with me.

'Anyone home,' I called. Nothing, I would have to go in.

Two steps along a corridor, I called out again. 'Sandra, I need to speak to you.' The smell of coffee and the pop of a percolator greeted me. Was the open door too helpful?

I crept the rest of the way into a kitchen. I saw her feet first. Then bare legs beneath a mini skirt. A girl lay sprawled out. Her blood swam across the floor from a crater in the back of her head, her brown hair was matted. I covered my mouth with my hand and pinched my nose. Thankfully the smell of coffee was thick on the air. I knew the blood would match that on the frantic woman's dress and now on Felix too. There was a stab in my heart; the girl's face matched my picture of Sandra.

Worse still, when the police answered her call, the woman would lead them straight to this room. I turned and ran, stumbled on the steps and grazed a shin, picked myself up and scurried onto the street.

No police, but further down the street, beyond my car, there was a huddle of people outside the pub. Damn, the woman had done just as I'd told her. How come Felix was involved with these crazy people? Was I being set up for a murder?

I ran to the car. A man appeared ahead of me, much stouter than Felix. Closer I could see that he had the boot of the Corsair open. I slowed and advanced. Please

Felix, have the sense to stay put, with the fedora pulled well down.

The man jerked upright on hearing me. His hair was slicked back and he had a moustache. His tie was askew and he had a wide-eyed look. Definitely some local toff.

I stubbed my fingers on the car door handle. Felix was already reaching across to unlock it.

'Where have you been?' I looked in at Felix but he shook his head. It was the toff who had spoken. No time for pleasantries, I ducked to get in. The door was torn from my grasp.

'I asked where you had been,' he stood above me.

'Just leaving, good night,' I fobbed him off.

'Where is she?' It was Felix.

'Not now,' I hissed. She'll follow on.

Who were these people? They could send this job to hell; the hysterical woman, the aggressive toff and Sandra dead on the floor.

The big man held the door so it wouldn't close.

'Clear off, or we'll get rough,' I tugged the door. Then he grabbed my arm. To stop falling sideways, I swung my feet out, and stood up fast.

'Get away.' When I shoved him his grip tightened on my wrist. Then I saw a length of pipe in his free hand. I tore at him and threw myself to the ground. It broke his grip and I rolled away. A clang told me that his blow had hit the car.

There was enough light to show a crazy grimace on his face. 'You were in my house.' He growled and advanced still holding the pipe. I pushed up and found my feet. Then with a shudder, I realised that I was fight-ing Sandra's killer. Her head had been burst open by this man. I was braced to tackle him when Felix appeared. 'Keep out of it, he's a killer,' I raged.

Felix had torn off his coat. I froze as he leapt and pulled it over the man's head and hung on. The pipe clanged to the ground as the man struggled to get free but Felix held on.

'Leave this to me.' A stern Felix dragged the man to the ground. I picked up the pipe and stood ready.

'Don't kill him,' I ordered. Two corpses on the same street could bring my mission to a nasty end.

He was kneeling on the man, totally in control. I glanced ahead to where the group of people muttered by the pub. Still no police, we'd been lucky but not for much longer.

When I turned back, Felix was standing on the bundle, his eyes ablaze.

'You are a most privileged spy to see this,' he announced. The coat settled a little beneath him.

'What the hell's going on, Felix?'

The breath whistled from his mouth as he pressed down. The bundle had ceased to struggle. Felix kept one foot in place. He pressed and his foot went lower, the bundle had shrunk.

The sweat ran down my back and I was panting but I couldn't take my eyes of the black shape on the ground. Felix turned to face me, his head like a statue staring, lifeless. Then he stood tall and stepped onto his coat with both feet.

'What's happening?' I croaked.

Suddenly he stepped back, bent and seized the coat with both hands. A matador's swish brought the coat over his shoulders and I followed his gaze back to the gritty paving stones... The toff had disappeared.

A Man of our Time

I felt like I was about to be attacked, but all I'd done was turn up for work late. Herman chatted to a blonde customer; heads bowed over a tube of tattoo goo. It looked like he'd inflicted his first work of the day on her shapely canvas. Perhaps he wouldn't notice me, on my toes.

'Ere, Stewart, you can take for this.'

I'd reached the till and had to do his bidding. It whirred as I ran a finger down the price list on the wall.

'What was it, Herman?'

'A butterfly.'

Another free spirit flutters into suburbia. 'Shoulder blade or arse?'

'Same price now.' He didn't pause from his patter about the healing powers of goo.

As the girl rooted in her handbag, my mind tripped over my years of work at uni. The disappointment tightened my stomach and my breath came in short bursts. Then a credit card was thrust in my face.

'It was my shoulder blade, actually.' She lent so close that I expected her forehead to butt my nose. I must have annoyed her. It's not often that my social skills are tested in the tattoo studio. When I handed her card back, I said. 'Try not to lie on your back for a few nights, it might hurt.'

She snatched her stuff, lasered me with blue eyes and bolted at the speed of a shop lifter.

Herman shook his head and muttered something about the Diplomatic Corps. I went to make coffee and left him to his needles and pins.

Herman's kitchen wasn't a place that cultivated every bacterium known to man; it was far worse than that. I flipped the kettle on and assessed my life. Here I was a qualified solicitor, struggling on the minimum wage. I thought about my sister, also skint, working for a church in Africa. At least she had sunshine. Perhaps we'd inherited the skint gene from our parents.

Herman, the creative, had given me the title, Admin Manager. A more accurate role would have been, 'Barista,' but that wouldn't look good on my CV.

'You out again tonight?' He asked as I handed over his 'Black Sabbath' mug.

I couldn't say - 'yes, I'm taking Magnolia out for dinner', without him thinking that he paid me too much.

'No, probably go around to Magnolia's place.'

He slurped his flat white, causing a wave to spill onto his scraggy trousers.

Truth was that Magnolia and I had to dig into our savings for nights out now. I switched on the computer and slumped in the chair with a shiver. How long would it take to get back to my world?

*

Magnolia and I skipped the starter, ordered the main course and started an argument.

'It's a publicity stunt,' I scoffed. The local builder was running a raffle for one of his new houses. 'It's to get everyone excited about the houses. Then the losers will be so disappointed that they'll buy one anyway.'

She rested her elbows on the table. 'You always knock everything. That's why you never get anywhere, you're a cynic.'

'Can't you see that you don't have a chance? He'll need to sell thousands of tickets to cover the price of a house? You've more chance of marrying Matt Damon than winning.'

'Thank you.' She took a gulp of wine and looked around the half empty place. 'Do you realise that you could get out of your stinking room and own your own home, for twenty pounds?'

'Twenty quid for a raffle ticket. You won't catch me throwing that sort of cash away. I could buy four bottles of wine for that.'

'I thought you wanted us to live together?' The waiters around the bar turned to stare at us, like a pride of alley cats.

'I do, and I've got that interview tomorrow. If I get the job, I'll be OK for a mortgage and we can move in together.'

She put her glass down on some precise spot on the tablecloth. 'This had better work Stewart. We've stood still for a year now, since you lost your last job.'

I put my glass down without precision, a drop of red wine fanned out on the linen. 'If you hadn't thrown up in the senior partner's Aston Martin, I'd still have a job.'

She gasped as if Matt Damon had walked in. The truth was that I was driving away from a party at the boss's manse, when Magnolia opened the window and thrust her head out. I braked, we were still in his drive and she chucked up his oysters and champagne into his Aston, parked with the hood down. I drove off in a panic but not before the office snitches had seen us.

'Don't blame me,' she snorted. It was your idea to get into his Jacuzzi earlier. If he hadn't caught us it wouldn't have been so bad.' Her teeth were bared, tainted red by the wine, but her eyes were tainted by her spirit.

'You didn't have the embarrassment of negotiating a reference.' It hadn't been an offence serious enough for dismissal, but it was better all round that I parted company with the practice. Our raised voices had stirred the alley cats by the bar. I smiled and nodded to them. Suddenly Magnolia's chair crashed to the floor and the wine bottle toppled. It gently rocked back and forth spewing red on the linen. She'd gone.

I held my head in my hands. Was it better to have loved and been caught in the Jacuzzi, than not to have loved at all?

*

At Parks Law, I was shown into the office of Melvin Park. A corner office with glass walls on two sides. Melvin looked like a lone guppy in an aquarium. If a giant be-speckled eleven-year-old had tapped on the glass outside, I would have gulped to please him.

'Stew...art, good to meet you.' He shook my hand while he faced the water cooler. Then he filled a real glass with spa water and presented it to me like it was a Golden Globe.

I clutched it and sat on an upright chair like a yoga teacher. Melvin settled in comfort and then we were off on script. My 2:1 law degree delighted him, and the fact that I'd completed the Legal Practice Course made him ooze. He slipped off script to tell me that Katherine Palmerstone-Smyth, Head of Negligence Claims, was in court, but her team would pulverise the other side, in time for her to join us.

I batted back my responses to him without touching the net. Beyond the windows an ambulance wailed through the streets and I wondered if Park's lawyers were already chasing it. I won my points and sipped his water but the big one was still to come. My hands were fluttering like butterflies, so I put the glass down and clutched them together.

'Why did you leave your last practice? I see it was over a year ago.'

I let a breath go by. I could have handed him the prepared script from my pocket, but I hung my arm over the back of the chair and said. 'It was a personal matter.' I could say anything I liked now. My previous employer would produce the brief reference that we'd agreed on. I went on, 'My sister was working for her church in Sierra Leone, handing out texts in the street. At the same time an anti -government group came along passing out leaflets. The police clashed with the politicos and my sister and friends were arrested along with them.'

Melvin leant forward; my sister's supposed plight etched into his brow.

'Well, our parents and I decided that I should go out there to help. So, I resigned my job.'

His mouth hung open. My performance was worthy of a Golden Globe.

'What happened,' he gasped.

'I managed to get her released.'

'What part did you play, Stewart?'

'I negotiated alongside the church leaders.'

'Is your sister home now?'

'No, she's still working out there, dedicated, you know,' I gave a nod.

'Well done.' He looked happy. Good result, Stewart- 1, World- Nil.

Then there was a rap on the door.

'This will be Katherine.'

We both stood and I straightened my tie, arranged a smile then turned to meet my next boss.

The sight of her sucked the breath from me. What was she doing here? The job, the house and Magnolia fluttered through the windows and away over the roof tops. It was the shapely blonde with the butterfly tattoo. On her shoulder blade as I recall. The aquarium was full of water; I couldn't hear what Parks was saying. I forced a heavy step toward Katherine and watched my hand float toward her.

Her mouth was open and her eyes wide, like she was drowning. When we touched, her hand recoiled like a turtle's head. Then I exhaled and my body weight came back with a thud.

'What's your current job?' Fresh from court, her blood was still at interrogation level.

I gulped and managed to keep the game going. 'I'm Admin Manager with a small organisation, Artistic Enterprises.' I blessed Herman for his creativity.

She turned down her volume and groped for a chair.

Perhaps it wasn't her. I looked for a small lump on her back but as she faced me, I couldn't see. It was wishful thinking; the scowl and laser blue eyes were unmistakable.

'Have you been involved in any work, other than legal?'

Parks tidied his papers and frowned.

Why should this happen to me? I nearly shouted *hell I just want to work*. Then I decided that I'd lost the job anyway, so if she wanted to talk tattoos, then she could bring it up. My head cleared and my thoughts became sharper.

'Actually, I did do something else. I resigned my last job to go to Africa. Then I repeated the story I'd told Parks. Katherine stared, hardly moving, except when she reached back to scratch her shoulder blade.

I finished, and left space for them to fill. My hands thought it was summer and wanted to flutter off and seek pollen. The creases left Katherine's brow and I realised that without them, she was quite a looker. Shame about the tattoo.

There was a noise in my head. Finally, they both shook my hand and smiled. I got out. End of story. She knew it was me but I had saved face. Magnolia would bounce off the walls if I told her what had happened. I needed to find another interview before I told her that this one had crashed.

*

Herman opened the shop door and sent a freshly pierced Goth on her way. He buried himself in the back room with the radio tuned to some 'long time ago station.'

I was engrossed with his junk computer when the door opened again, but instead of the graveyard Goth, I faced Magnolia. What did she want?

'Sorry about the other night,' she mumbled.

She obviously wanted to make up.

'I've been thinking. What's the latest on that job?'

'Still waiting to hear.' I shrugged, like this was normal.

'Well I'm not.' I thought she might stamp a foot. Could she be going to ...dump me?

'What?' I tried.

'It's over, Stewart. I've had enough. We're not going anywhere and you mess up all the time.'

Her mess on the Aston's soft, supple upholstery had been forgotten.

'Do you understand, Stewart?'

I looked from her watery eyes to the floor and back. I had no prospects to offer her. A bus drove by and rattled the windows. One day the dump would fall down and it looked like I'd still be in it.

'If you're sure that's what you want,' I said.

'There's no point,' she sobbed. Then turned and went the way of the bleeding Goth.

Slumped in the chair with Herman's rock pioneers hammering on my anvils, I thought about me. Since I'd met Magnolia everything had caved in. Was this place to be my fate? Without a job, I was trapped and now I'd lost my girlfriend.

I had to get out of the place. Go anywhere. If I could afford a ticket, I'd book a trip on 'Mars One'. Or perhaps I could go along for free, and work as their 'Barista'.

*

Days later, I still hadn't applied to 'Mars One', when Herman shoved a newspaper in front of me. I saw Magnolia's picture but couldn't believe what I read.

'I can't believe what I'm reading,' I gasped.

'Off the wall that one, I warned you.'

I cringed and read on. Magnolia had won the builders raffle and was the proud owner of a new house. She stood on the front step accepting the keys from a Matt Damon look-a-like. The presentation had taken place the day before she dumped me. On the way home, I spent twenty quid on four bottles of wine, Mars -1, Stewart- Nil.

*

The day after my wine therapy the diary was clear and Herman was out. The shop flashed from sunlight to shade as the traffic passed the windows. Each flash hurt my eyes. More nausea flowed through me when I saw the email from Melvin Parks. At least he hadn't left me in doubt about the job for the rest of my days. The 'elbow' was about to be applied in writing. What a gent.

He'd written a lot. I could have dumped someone myself in a single sentence. There were attachments too; Contract of Employment, Phone Policy, Travel Policy, and Policies for nit-picking policies. Damn it, he'd only given me the job!

If only Magnolia had waited.

*

I'd been at Parks Law about a week when Katherine took me to a meeting with clients.

'I need you to back me up.' She was a beauty when she smiled.

The meeting ended late and when the clients had gone, Katherine pushed her chair back from the document strewn table and sighed. She sank back into the chair and closed her eyes. I let her enjoy the peace.

'I'm so glad you joined us, Stewart,' she purred.

This was promising. I was still relieved at there having been no mention of the tattoo studio.

'I know how bad it must have been for you working in that tattoo place.' She opened her eyes.

My stomach fluttered. Oh hell, what do I say now?

'This is in confidence,' she went on.

The flutters dropped to half flap and I sat back.

'You see, I have a problem like yours.'

'What's my problem?' I thought I'd got over them. Even the tattoo studio had just gone public.

'My brother is in prison in Latvia,' she spoke quietly, 'accused of smuggling their precious amber.'

'What?'

'I need your help, Stewart. You got your sister freed from Sierra Leone. I'm desperate and you know what to do.

Back in Tennessee

Ben slid the menu across the table and scanned the southern fare. He decided on a steak, then sat back and checked the occupants of the gas station diner. There were two girls on the tills at the front. He would ask them later if they knew his old friend. Three truckers yelled at a baseball game on TV and munched popcorn, but passing trade was of no interest to Ben.

'How ya all.' The waitress was blonde, and wore an orange uniform dress. She set down a bowl of popcorn and a napkin that matched her uniform, and then scribbled down his order with a pen plucked from her hair. She was good for her age, thought Ben, as he felt the stubble on his chin and hand combed his fading red hair.

The place had changed so much. It had been no more than a timber shed and a single pump, but now there were lines of pumps and a concrete and glass building. He could see down the length of the room and out through the front windows, where the red maples stood dark across the Interstate. It felt good to relax in his home county, but he'd need to get on with his search early the next day.

Soon the waitress cut into his thoughts as she stooped to set the food down. He saw in her face, pencil black eyebrows above soft green eyes and there was a trace of a scar on her right cheek. As she swung away, he wasn't sure, and stopped himself from calling her back.

He left his food untouched and turned to keep her in view as she strutted to the truckers table. The years had changed her, but he would never forget her eyes and the scar was the one made by a tennis racket at High School. He just knew it. Hell, it's Jodie, what's she doing working here? What were the chances of meeting like this?

She was the reason for his visit, but it was too soon, it would be difficult. How could he talk here? He bent his head and stared at his plate until the griddle burns on the steak swam, and the heat reached his face and added to his sweat. Fancy her working as a waitress. Damn. He concentrated on cutting his steak. He ate, his fork rapidly spiking the chunks of meat. The food turned to pulp in his mouth and he breathed heavily. The smell of disinfectant reached his nostrils as Jodie wiped tables, and exchanged banter with the truckers. He was convinced now it was her, a bit heavier, but years of southern fried food would have done that.

With a bored expression, she came back toward him. The bright lights seemed to dim and all he could hear was the hum of the chiller cabinets in the store. He swallowed some coke. Come on talk to her, she can only curse and snub you.

'How ya doin back here, can we get ya anything else?' It was Jodie's face but fuller and lines from her eyes traced a smile. It was because he was staring, that her brow wrinkled and she focused on him. The sight of his teenage girlfriend made his heart thump and the blood whistle in his ears.

'Ben'. She gasped, and bent closer.

He smiled, but felt himself lean away from her. No doubt about it now. Careful what you say to her.

'For God's sake. Where have you been?' Then she clasped her hands together and laughed. 'I guess that's a dumb question after so long.'

'I was just passing, on the way to Nashville. Thought I must call in but didn't expect to see you here.' He laughed. He wasn't ready to tell her that he'd come looking for her.

'I bet you didn't.' She pulled at the front of her dress and hid some cleavage. 'I guess you'd have just driven by if you'd known.' Her smile went out.

'No, it's good to see you, after so long. How is everything?'

Then she slid her arm around his neck and hugged him. He felt her hair soft on his face. When she pulled back, he studied her. He'd agonised over how he'd greet her; they had been so close. It felt good that she had taken over, and been affectionate.

She sat down and faced him. 'Whoa, it's over twenty years. Where do I start?' As she collected her thoughts, she clasped her arms about herself and beamed at him.

Is she going to bring up the past or let it be?

'Well I got married.' She waited for him to catch up.

Pretty safe bet, he thought. 'That's good, anyone I know?' He held a hand to his mouth to conceal his heavy breathing.

'You don't know him, he came along later,' she said quietly.

Ben felt the blood tingle down his arms to his fingers.

'Well that's nice. Do you have any kids?'

'Two boys, in their twenties now,' she said with a smug smile. 'How about you Ben?'

He swallowed, kids twenty years old, had he left her pregnant? 'I'm married ten years, but there's just the two of us.'

27

'No kids then?' She raised an eyebrow. 'Where are you living?'

'Maryland, but I've been all over.'

'Looks like you're doing OK.' She nodded to his suit.

That's country folk, Ben thought, if you're not wearing jeans, you stand out like a vegetarian at a hog roast.

'I built up my own business. We work across the south.'

'So, what brought you back here and so late in the evening?' Her head was on one side, streaks of hair feathered her forehead.

'I'm setting up a business operation in Memphis. I had a meeting there, so Interstate 40 brought me back, and work made me this late.' He looked down at his plate. They needed to warm to each other, before he could open up.

As she nodded the pen slipped from her hair, quickly she caught it and shoved it back.

The grill chef called out, 'Jodie, I need ya to look at something for me.'

'I'll be back.' Ben watched as she wriggled out of the booth and crossed to the counter.

So, she's got kids and from twenty years back. When he looked down to his hands, he saw shreds of orange napkin in his lap. He hadn't expected to have feelings. He'd thought of her over the years. How it could have been, if they'd stayed together. Minutes passed and he shuffled in his chair. Then he craned back, to see where she was. The chef came out the back with an order. The door was open long enough for him to catch sight of Jodie on a cell phone.

He had a smile in place when she squeezed back into the seat. It was time to clear up the past.

'Tell me, how did the guy working here that night, get along afterwards?' He'd lowered his voice.

She looked down her nose.

Ben went on talking. 'I mean was he OK, I couldn't find out.'

'The guy you shot lived, if that's what you came back for. In fact, we all did. No one got caught. No one died. And no one did time. We all lived happily ever after.' Her eyes glistened.

In the silence a truck hammered down the Interstate, with a blast from its air horns.

I must keep her talking. Ben looked down at the back of Jodie's right hand. The skin was like a wrinkled tomato, a gold band and a diamond caught the light. He felt he'd lost. Her man had done well.

'How's everyone else?' This is like opening a coffin, I don't want to look in but I just have to.

'Well, Sam got together with Crystal and Jake married Tilley. Mathew got a job with the Government.' Her lips had curled into a familiar smile, like the old Jodie.

That accounts for the rest of the gang, all still stuck here. He couldn't worry about them.

'I need a smoke. D'ya still smoke, Ben?'

He nodded and checked his watch. He'd have to wait this out, too soon to ask a favour.

'Come on.' She led the way. Ben rose slowly from his seat, grimaced and rubbed his back before following.

They moved away from the shop front and stood by a wall in the shadows. Ben pulled out a pack of Dunhill's and flipped away his doctor's warnings. He put two in his mouth, lit them and handed her one. She leant forward and took it from him with her mouth. Her lips brushed his fingers and set his nerves tingling. An owl hooted in the woods behind the building.

'Are you happy then?' He saw the smoke from her mouth curl in the cool air.

'Yes. I made a bit of money, got a ranch house with a couple of horses. That's my Lincoln over there.' The red tip of his cigarette zig- zagged in the dark.

She took another pull of smoke. 'I asked if you were happy. Not how rich you are.'

'Well, fine.'

'But it would be better with kids. Her fault I guess.'

He looked at her closely before he answered. 'It's OK, you know what it's like, and I work a lot.' He spoke sharply.

'Me too, where are you staying tonight?'

'Hotel in Nashville, I'm meeting clients in the morning.' He drew hard and filled his lungs, to cover the lie. There were no clients.

'You could have stayed here. When the oil company took over, they built cabins, by the lake at the back. We're a motel now. Come and take a look.'

Before Ben could answer, she walked to the corner of the building. He followed with his back bent; smoke billowed behind them. Go along with it; stick with her, he thought.

Around the back, it took seconds before he could see Jodie's orange dress ahead of him in the dark. She had taken a path through the maples.

It was difficult to remain steady as he followed over the uneven ground, a broken ankle wouldn't help. Closer to the lake, he felt a chill in the air and drew his jacket collar around him. When he saw the flat surface reflecting the moon, he felt a pang of regret. It felt good to be back in Tennessee.

Jodie had stopped by the water's edge near a cluster of cabins. He saw her cigarette butt arc into the water. As he caught up, he saw light from the building glint in her eyes. Back in the parking lot, a car pulled up and a door slammed. Ben turned to look in the direction of the sounds.

It's a set up. She's set me up and I fell for it. That's why she was on the phone. Enticed me round the back and now the hicks have come to get their own back.

'Look, Jodie, I need to leave soon, but I'll be around here more now. I'd like to see you again.' He looked back the way they had come and reached for the comfort of his cell phone.

'You've got all nervous, Ben. Wanting to leave, but then you're good at getting scared and running out on me. Aren't you?'

Ben could hear voices, men laughing and calling out. Damn, now she wants to go over all that. This could ruin everything.

Then Jodie poked a finger at his chest. 'I didn't know where you'd gone back then. I was sick for months when you disappeared. I didn't know whether you were hurt or dead.' Her voice carried through the night.

'I was young,' he stammered.

'And ruthless, that's why you're such a big shot now, compared to us.'

'I couldn't come back. I was scared. I thought the guy I shot in the gas station might be dead.'

'You're getting old Ben, over forty, aren't you? Want to clear your conscience before you meet God?'

'Don't forget there were four of us, not just me.'

'Big difference was Ben, that you took a shooter and used it on a kid your own age. Then you ran out on your friends and the foster-parents who'd taken you out of the orphanage. Your disappearing killed them; you know. You took the money too. Your business has grown out of dirty money. Do your new friends know that?'

He raised his hand. 'What happened at this gas station all those years ago, just terrified me, I had to get out.'

She was still, her features like ice. Ben heard a vehicle moving and shot a glance behind him.

'You called your husband from the kitchen back there, didn't you?'

Suddenly her body loosened up, her shoulders sagged and she started to laugh. 'You are a first-class creep. You only worry about yourself. You didn't even think about me. I guess you are suddenly worried about what happened back then, because you're going to work in this state and now you want to clear your old mess up first.'

Ben's fists clenched and he glared at her. She'd ruined his plans. He couldn't ask tonight, not now. He'd have to come back again.

'Look Jodie, it was a long time back and I'd change it if I could, but I can't. Let's stay friends.' As he turned to leave, he pulled out his phone, and glanced ahead to the parking lot. Jodie drew alongside.

'You better tell whoever you called, to leave off me. I can cause them a hell of a lot of heart ache if they step out of line.'

Jodie gave a brittle laugh.

'What's so funny then?' He tried to keep up with her but stumbled. He slowed down; they would reach the parking lot at any minute.

'The heart ache will be all yours, believe me.' Her words were cut from ice.

Ben braced himself as they turned the corner of the building into the bright lights. He saw a pickup with a driver inside, but there was no gang of hicks ready to beat him up. He looked at Jodie.

She grimaced and grabbed his arm. The driver got out, a young man dressed in jeans, a check shirt and a cowboy hat. A real hick if ever I saw one, thought Ben.

'Ready to go when you are Ma,' he called to Jodie.

'Be with you in a minute Kyle, just showing a customer round.'

The young man took off his hat to reveal a mop of red hair. 'Good evening sir.' He gave a broad smile to Ben, and climbed back into the cab.

Jodie clutched Ben's hand and looked up at him. Tears ran down her cheeks. 'I thought it was an opportunity for you, to see your son.'

She ran a hand across her face and rushed to climb into the truck. Ben didn't move. He just stared at the pickup. Kyle reversed and as they sped away, waved his hat from the window, Ben stood like a lone tree, his mouth hung open, but his mind raced.

The noise of the engine tailed off down the highway, like a spent sky rocket. Ben felt that much more than a pickup truck had just left him. Then a smile tickled his face and he raised both hands. 'I've done it,' he said aloud. His quest wasn't over but the success so far sent him hobbling to the Lincoln.

In the driver's seat he scribbled down the registration number of Kyle's truck and grabbed his cell phone. He turned up his doctor's number and the phone whirred. He clutched the wheel with his free hand and stamped his feet. When a gruff voice answered, Ben spoke quickly. 'Doctor Parini, Its Ben Holden. I'm in Tennessee, and I've found a blood relation. I have a son'

Hat Trick

Alf stepped back and admired his moustache in the cracked mirror, the close shave had made it more notice-able. He smiled, made a gun of his fingers and shot his reflection.

Now for the jelly in the doughnut, the bourbon in the coffee.

He shrugged on his father's overcoat and topped the ensemble with the trilby hat he'd stolen from a clothing store the day before.

'Here comes the boy,' he spoke to the mirror, 'Alf becomes Alphonse, Chicago's newest gangster.'

His mother's wireless was blasting out 'Over the Rainbow' as he opened the kitchen door. She sat at the table peeling potatoes into a copy of the Chicago Tribune.

'Ciao Ma, I'm going out.'

'Not so fast, let me see you.' She was slim and although not yet forty, lines radiated from her bright eyes.

He smiled, and waited while she looked over his clothes.

'You look good in your Pa's coat but where did you get the hat.

''Err, it's on the tab for now but I'll pay it off soon, don't worry.'

'But I do worry about you Alf. You be careful running up bills. If you don't pay, you'll get into trouble.'

'What's for dinner?' He moved to stand behind her, one hand on her shoulder. Her hair was brown with just a few strands of grey.

'Potato pie, I'll put something tasty in too, like chilies.'

'Great, look forward to that,' he bent and kissed the top of her head. She didn't turn, so missed the fondness in his smile.

'Where are you going, all dressed up?'

'Just a bit of business, Ma. I'll make some money for us soon.'

'I'll look forward to that,' she beamed.

He moved to the door. It worried him that she stayed home so much since his father's death. Why did he, out of all the workmen, have to fall from the top floor of the Hilton Towers? He hated to think about the cruel blow to his family.

He stepped onto the landing, closed the door and at once inhaled the familiar smells of cat pee and boiled cabbage. He'd had a great idea. It meant he could settle with the loan shark and at the same time earn a reputation as a hustler. The other boys his age always laughed at his talk about getting rich but they would still be working in the brewery when he was enjoying the good life.

While he clattered down flights of stairs, he rehearsed the lines he would use to scam the bar owner. 'I work for Mr Bezani, he needs no introduction, does he? We give a good service, keep your business safe so you can ...' He'd reached the first floor and stopped speaking to himself because a square man ahead blocked the doorway to the street.

As he walked up, his shoulders sagged and he felt sweat around the hat's band. He didn't ask the man to move but tried to slide around his bulk. He was almost there when a gloved hand shot out and grabbed him by the throat. Alf croaked and spluttered then fell back pinned to the wall.

'Think I wouldn't recognise you under that hat O'Malley?'

It's Bezani and I haven't got his money. He's gonna kill me. Just when I was sorting things out.

'Mr Bezani. No, I'm not trying to hide from you,' he held up his hands.

'Oh sure, you just put on a disguise to go to the movies or something.'

'No, no I'm working. Gonna get your money.'

'Thanks for bringing that up kid. It had slipped my mind, standing here in these beautiful surroundings.'

'I'll get it Mr Bezani, just give me a bit more time.'

Please, just a few days.

'Don't make me laugh, you keep on lying and not shelling out. Perhaps I should go upstairs and shoot your Ma, serve as a reminder to ya.'

Oh no, not Ma, he doesn't mean this. He's just tormenting me.

'Look coupla days that's all I need. Then you'll be paid up with interest and all.'

'In a couple more days it'll be fifty bucks, you get it wise guy?' Bezani brought his knee up quickly, it ploughed into Alf like a hammer paralysing his leg. When Bezani let him go, he dropped to the floor. His trilby rolled through the doorway and across the sidewalk into the path of a horse and cart. It was brought to a halt by the clump of a hoof.

*

He reached the bar mid-afternoon and got to the basement washroom without seeing anyone. The trilby no longer sat right, he felt more like Stan Laurel than a gangster. His eyes were wide and he sneezed in the chill of the place.

Why did Bezani have to show up? He's ruined everything.

He splashed water on his face. *I don't feel like this now.*

He rehearsed his lines to the mirror. 'I work for Mr Bezani...' but his voice dried up and he had to drink tainted water from a squeaky tap.

I must make this work. There's nothing else for me and Ma. There are no jobs, only in the stinking brewery.

After fifteen minutes locked in a cubicle he walked out to the bar. The warm air smelt of cigars and stale beer. A boy a little older than himself sang along to 'South of the Border' as he cleaned tables. Alf stopped dead a distance from him, swallowed and dug his hands into the overcoat pockets.

I feel like an idiot now. It felt so right before. I should leave, go home and drink a coffee with Ma. But what if Bezani turns up again. I got to make this work.

He cleared his throat and forced his leaden feet a few steps toward the boy. 'Hey, you, I work for Mr Bezani, he needs no introduction, does he?'

The boy scowled and straightened up.

Oh hell, he's built like a football player. Alf fingered a button on his coat.

'What?' the boy demanded.

He doesn't get it, what now?

The boy threw down the cloth he was using.

Alf felt his shoulders twitch. 'Bezani sent me', he snarled. 'You guys have been getting away with it too long, understand?'

'No,' the boy crossed his arms and smirked.

'You're not paying your dues and if you want to stay in business, you start paying for security now. Get it?'

'No, we never have trouble here, it's a good neighbourhood.'

'You dope, what I'm saying is you will have trouble if you don't pay up,' Alf heard his voice squeak to the empty room.

The boy dropped his hands to his sides and stepped forward. 'You want protection money?'

He's going to punch me.

'Look,' Alf shook, 'don't mess with Bezani, he'll close you down.' He stepped back from the boy. 'He wants fifty bucks by the end of the week,' his chest heaved, there was a sound behind the bar, another boy had appeared from the back room.

There's two of them, they'll kill me.

'What's he want?' the new comer growled.

'He'll tell ya,' the first boy shrugged.

Alf made to leave. 'Fifty bucks by the end of the week, we'll be back,' His voice wavered, then he clattered up the stairs.

*

Alf hung around the apartment the next day reading the papers over and over and sighing a lot.

Those guys need teaching a lesson. I need help, some back up but the kids around here are happy to work like dogs and pay union dues. I can do better than that. Working didn't do my Pa any good.

The solution kept coming back to him and for a while he pushed it away. He'd figured out that nothing less than a gun would scare the bar owners in to paying up. He knew that pieces were traded from the back of an auto-mechanics nearby. Someone had told him that three dollars was the going rate for a handgun.

It took a day to find the money and then the guts to go over there. He stood outside fingering the bank notes in his pocket.

What do I say, what if the dealer isn't in? He buttoned his coat and pulled the hat brim down. *I'll just have to walk in, look around and size them up.*

There was no one at the front counter but he could see mechanics in blue overalls working beyond a glass screen. A few customers stood nearby so he pushed his way into the back and walked up to a Ford with its hood open. he breathed deeply on the smells of engine oil and gasoline. The workshop reflected in the panels, and he could see that no one had noticed him.

What now. I want a gun; I can't ask a mechanic. Rooted to the floor he stared at the black sheen of the paint job and the stitching of the upholstery. *Can't stay here, got to move.*

There was a door half open in the wall behind the car, he stepped lightly toward it. Inside a huge man lounged at a desk. After a deep breath Alf pushed open the door. He jumped when a whippet yapped loudly at him, it strained on a rope attached to a filing cabinet.

The man's square face turned, 'sharrup,' he growled at the dog. Alf could smell sweat and peppermint gum.

'You the owner?'

'Yep. Fastest dog in the world.'

'I meant, of this place,' Alf said.

'Yep too.'

There followed a silence. *Calm down, calm down, ask him straight.*

Alf squared his shoulders. 'Friends tell me I can buy a handgun around here.'

The man leant back in his chair. Alf turned his face away as the man studied him from shoes to crushed hat. Then the mountain settled into his chair. 'What sort dya want?'

'Semi-automatic.'

The dealer looked down at papers in front of him.

'OK, what about ammo?'

'Yes please. Err, one magazine.'

The dealer sighed and slid open a desk drawer, pulled out a ring of keys, then dragged himself over to a walk-in-safe. His chest heaved as he pulled open the door. 'Hold it there,' he held up a palm as Alf moved closer.

It's working, I'm getting the gun, that'll scare them.

The dealer puffed his way out, his hands clutched the pieces to his chest, he back heeled the door shut.

'Look at that, three pieces,' Alf exclaimed.

They were laid on the desk side by side, black steel barrels pointing the same way, butts shabby with use. There was a feint smell of gun oil.

'Ya know what you're looking at kid?'

'Best tell me.'

The dealer pointed a finger at each gun in turn. 'That's a Colt 1911, a Smith and Wesson and another Colt, the newest of the bunch.'

'How much is it?'

'The newer one's ten dollars and I'll let the other two go for eight dollars apiece. Full magazine is a dollar extra.'

Alf gulped, licked his lips and picked up the Colt. He spread his feet and held the gun out in front of him.

I'm unstoppable. It's great, feels like there's a wall around me.

The dealer was back in his chair. Tools clattered on the floor outside and a voice cursed.

'Would ya take a deposit?' Alf asked quietly.

The block head spun to face him, 'What? What did you say?'

Oh no, he doesn't want to.

'I could leave a deposit, pay the rest later,' he croaked.

'How much you got?'

Alf put the gun down, his hand left sweat on the butt. 'Three bucks.'

The man sighed again and shook his head from side to side. 'No credit, come back when you're flush.' He collected up the guns.

'OK, I'll be back.' Alf felt his face burn red.

Who the hell told me three dollars? What can I do now? He shuffled out into the garage area and made to leave.

'Stop him, stop that guy.' Alf turned not realising that the voice meant him.

'He stole from me.' A man in a suit strode toward him. 'That's him alright, he stole that hat he's wearing from my store.'

'Get him.' The bellow sent three heavy weight mechanics in pursuit as Alf fled. He was out in the street and well ahead when he heard the excited bark of the whippet. The fastest dog in the world snapped at his ankles then got between his legs and tripped him. He hit the floor face first and tasted blood. The dog danced excitedly around him and nipped his ear. Alf cried out and punched at air. Moments later a mound of blue overalls fell on him and held him while the store keeper wrestled the three dollars from his pocket then walked away whistling.

Oh hell. I almost got it. He took my money, what do I do now?

*

Alf stopped at the top of the basement stairs to shrug his coat back square on his shoulders. The starting pistol he'd bought weighed heavy and he felt untidy with the plaster covering his ear lobe. The stairs were empty, but the bar below gurgled with the sound of drinkers.

Why can't I have money too, why do I have to be broke all the time. His first step was heavy. *What if they say no again? What will I do? Damn Bezani.* Smoke funnelled up from below and caught his breath. He shrugged again to level his shoulder pads then straightened up.

It's tough but I must be like the gangsters, rule this neighbourhood. He marched down the stairs.

There were more people in the dimly lit bar than he wanted. He pulled the brim of his hat down; rivulets of sweat were already streaking his face. He had to get this over smartish.

One of the owners laughed with a girl as he shook a cocktail. The other boy emerged from beneath the bar with a beer bottle in each hand. Neither of them paid any attention to Alf.

'Hey, give us a beer over here,' he called.

Both heads turned toward him, then the nearest boy nodded to the other.

'Over here,' Alf called again.

The boy with the beers placed one bottle in front of him.

'I'll take the fifty dollars now too.' He whispered and stared the boy in the eye.

The boy nodded and turned to his partner who moved into the back room. Alf held his glass close when he drank, to stop his coat falling open with the weight of the pistol. *Hurry up for chrissake.*

A big man with a cane pushed up to the bar and rapped his fist for attention. Alf forced himself alongside the man and leant forward to see what was keeping the boys.

'Gerrout of it.' The man shoved him. Alf toppled backwards into a drinker who stepped out of the way, he lost his balance and fell to the floor. A thud on the boards then a sudden lightness in his coat told him he'd lost the starting pistol.

'Let me up, let me up.' Legs like tree trunks penned him in.

Someone's going to stand on me, where's the damn gun?' He scrabbled on his knees over cigarette butts and spilt beer. His hat was knocked off but he saw the glint of the metal gun and scuttled toward it.

'What's that guy doing?' People pushed and shoved, then a girl screamed, 'He's got a gun.'

His hand was on the butt when a boot stamped on it.

'Oh no, let me up,' but the boot stayed put. He tugged hard but remained anchored to the floor.

'Let me go, let me go,' he shouted, 'I'm not going to hurt anyone.'

Then a shove sent him flat out but he still held onto the gun. Suddenly a face twisted with fear appeared above him. One of the bar tenders bellowing. Alf saw that he held a sawn-off shot gun.

'Don't shoot me', he clutched his fake pistol.

The crowd shouted and screamed as they fled. Feet pounded the floor like thunder around him. 'No, no,' he cried. There was a woof of air and a terrific bang when the gun went off then shot peppered him.

Alf's face was splattered with blood, it soaked his moustache. His head flopped down on the boards. His last thought was of his Ma waiting alone in the apartment with his dinner spoiling in the oven.

The bar tender's eyes darted. He turned a strained face to the man with the cane, still at the bar. The shotgun shook in his hands. 'He wanted protection money,' the boy cried out.

'Sure,' said the man, 'look at him, he's one of those no-good gangsters. You did the right thing.'

Paradise Lost

I slid the rifle from its case and winced at the metallic clicks, but the African in the front seat of my Range Rover was not distracted from his mobile phone. He should expect to hear the clink of metal, because I'd faked a breakdown, so that I could stop on the bush road and blow his brains out.

The rifle was ready. The casino I would drive to alone was still miles ahead. The pulse of crickets electrified the night. Now, I had to get him out in the open. I didn't want his DNA splattered all over the upholstery. There was a flutter in my chest, like a butterfly in a jar.

When Josh finished his call, I shuffled away toward some trees. He could see me in the backwash from the headlamps, but couldn't see my clenched teeth. I needed him to catch up; he should have no qualms about following his trusted accountant into the blackness on a lonely road.

'Where you goin?' He growled from his seat.

When I reached cover I called, 'Look at this,' then dropped out of sight into the foliage. Hunkered down it was hard to breath. Would he take my bait?

'What you seen?'

I grasped the gun and kept my mouth shut.

There was a click as the door opened, I clutched the rifle across my body and jerked when a reggae ring tone broke the silence, Josh the busy man, had another phone call. Through the leaves I saw the door close and

51

cursed mobile phones, they cause more poverty in Africa than the tsetse fly.

I waited to kill the man who was a cop, a bent cop who'd taken everything that was bad and shaped it to suit his place in a tropical hell hole.

He had control of bars, and dealt in drugs and prostitution and on occasions needed an accountant to provide respectable figures. He owned people, but not me, although in the company of his government cronies, he would pat me on the back like a pet poodle. I pretended not to notice the winks and sniggers. In such company, a fifty-year-old European keeps his thoughts to himself, if he has plans to flit to London.

His execution wasn't just to please an honest accountant who'd got into bad company, this was for Lucy. Poor Lucy. Weeks after her disappearance her sister walked into my office, her shell eyes wide and damp.

'She's dead Mr Mac, they murdered her.'

'You know this, are you sure?' my voice wavered, and I swallowed hard.

'We've heard from friends who work in the government offices, people talk, and it gets back to us.'

I never saw Lucy or her sister again.

Now, my stomach churned, I wanted to wrench the Range Rover door open and blast him where he sat, but instead I had to turn my face to the sky and focus on the sparkle of the Southern Cross. After this, things would be better. A fresh start in UK and I'd sleep without strangling the sheets and scheming.

'Don't hassle her man, a girl as beautiful as her will do well with influential friends.' I wanted to beat Josh's big-toothed smile, but truth was his cronies would dump my body in the bush for the hyenas.

He called out to me, now several paces away from the Rover.

'Where are you Alex, what you found?'

It was a good place to drop him, but the light breeze was behind me, I gave myself a mental kick, I was hunting man not game.

He would have his police issue pistol close to hand. So, I called out in Swahili, to make him feel safe, we used the lingua franca, like friends.

Even so he stopped, a silhouette in the headlamps.

Come on come on, don't turn back; my hands were damp on the barrel and the trigger. I had to do it, no excuses.

Then his small figure shambled toward me. Strange, evil should be bigger.

I stood up. 'Here, what do you think of this Josh?' My mouth had dried. It had to be done. Why was a hesitating?

He slowed, his right-hand wavering. I'd spooked him.

A waterfall in my ears blotted out his answer.

Then he stopped, head forward, like a leopard about to spring.

Fear crashed over me. I wanted to turn and run. Suddenly his hand whipped inside his jacket.

The rifle bucked, a clumsy shot from the waist.

His screech fouled the night and tarnished the stars. I was bent over the gun, frozen. This was no gazelle; his screams tore into me. 'You went for your gun,' I yelled, 'it's your fault'.

A bomb exploded in my head. I'd shot him. I straightened, but Josh was still on his feet, one hand clutched to his chest. By the time I yanked the rifle round he'd staggered out of sight.

I broke cover to see him lumber into the bush to my left. Terror thrust me into the foliage. If I lost him now, I would be lucky to see the dawn never mind London.

Branches whacked my face and hands. Blood ran and my face stung. Birds flapped from their perches and flew into the night, but I ploughed on, in the darkness, my skin prickly for his bullet.

Nothing. Empty woods, my thrashing about had cost me the prey. He'd left me to run riot while he lay still somewhere, now he could work on his survival, and he still had his phone. He could be texting his men right now. How could I hide from them? How would I get out of this damn country?

I ran through the bush without direction. I stumbled, then fell and ran on again. The moon was backlighting the leaves like the midday sun. A thwack from a branch made me cry out, my temple ran wet.

It was a relief to see the lights of the Range Rover. I stooped at the place where I'd shot him, the ground was wet, he was losing blood and now it was on my hands.

The casino was the nearest place for miles; I had to get there. If Josh had enough life left, he would head there too. I'd be waiting.

I wiped my hands on a rag, shoved the gun into its case and dropped into the driver's seat. A few minutes' drive and the eyes of another car began to jog in the rear-view mirror. Fear forced my foot down and I bumped and lurched over the broken ground. Josh might get a lift from other gamblers on the road. My plan had gone to hell. What could I say if they questioned me for shooting a police officer? I cringed;

they'd say I was a common killer. Closer now, the car's headlamps flooded the interior; it could be a police vehicle that he'd called. I'd be shot in the bush without a chance. I took fright and pulled over.

They came up, faces at the windows. I sank into the seat and took deep breaths my hands clutched the wheel, my eyes watered. Music boomed, their headlamps flared, I was lit up like Macbeth on a stage. Then the light began to fade, and the African night took over, the pulse of the crickets and the shuffle of creatures. It was the bigger animal that I dreaded, dangerous when wounded and as sly as a hyena.

He must be behind me, or dead on the ground, there was no way of telling. I swivelled left and right. Minutes dragged I had to wait; he might just catch up to me.

I told myself it was for Lucy. Lucy my lovely assistant, she was all I had dreamt of. I'd become parched and cynical, my 20 years in Africa had begun to show. The adventure was over, the mire of corruption and scorching days in the decaying city had got to me. It was all easy to see now. How had I walked past the starved and diseased for all those years, keying numbers into computers and banking fees?

Lucy had turned stacks of paper into files, plants appeared on my office window ledges and the aroma of coffee greeted me on sunny mornings.

I flew her out to meet clients at the coast and to the coffee plantations up country, we became lovers and I returned to paradise. Until Josh the bent cop, came around to collect his creative accounting. He took my Lucy too.

The bush road would get busier as the night people searched for their luck; some well-meaning soul could stop and offer me help. I didn't want to be witnessed lurking in the dark, so I started the engine and turned back to search for Josh.

It was better moving; the lights dipped and fell and occasionally, the diamond eyes of a bat-eared-fox stared back.

Then suddenly he was there, close to the road arms flaying. I almost drove past him. I braked hard. The gun case wasn't locked, but I fumbled with the catch and finally wrenched the gun out with a curse, as I kept my night eyes on the prey. Ready to fire, I marched stiffly toward him. He was on his knees retching like a consumptive beggar.

My hands shook. I could help him to his feet, tell him it was all a mistake. His death gurgle made the bile rise to my throat. 'Lucy, Lucy, Lucy,' I bawled.

Last chance. I fought back the revulsion and aimed from the shoulder Eyes almost closed I squeezed the trigger and pledged to the African bush that it would be the last time. The very last time. That I would shoot one of its creatures.

He pitched forward and shuddered a moment, then lay still. The shot resounded. At last I'd done it. Would they hear it at the casino? My tortured mind flashed back to Lucy's gentle smile, as she stroked my dogs.

There was no joy in me when I locked the rifle away, just numbness. Then somehow survival kicked in.

The doorman frowned as I scuttled past. A glance over my shoulder showed him gaping.

In the men's room, a clean-up left a cut at my temple and scratches on my face. Shirt and jacket showed signs of my scrabble through the bush and my hands jumped each time the door opened.

I needed a drink, a few people to see me, to prove I'd been drinking alone. Then I could go home. Home to the bark of dogs, a locked door, and a guard at my gate.

A double scotch went quickly. The raw spirit stung without comfort. As I ordered the second, I caught sight of the doorman hovering. He was speaking to someone outside the bar. I kept my eyes on my glass as the chatter increased. If they came for me, I'd say that Josh had attacked me as I drove. We rolled out the car and my gun went off by accident. Surely, they'd believe me, I was respected, an honest accountant, no case against me.

I stiffened when a hand tapped my shoulder, I couldn't move, then I placed the glass firmly on the bar and turned. Had I botched the shot? Would it be Josh, bloodied and supported by his men? Was my plan in tatters? Was my destiny London, or to swing from a rope in Africa?

I turned.

There were two of them, Africans wearing black suits and grave faces. The nearest moved closer, his eyes level with mine, I flinched from the smell of his acid sweat and last cigarette.

'You are, Alex McCloud?' He didn't wait for an answer. 'I'm arresting you for the murder of Lucy Odendo. My insides sank. My vision blurred, and I stammered. 'Lucy, you've found Lucy?' I gagged and gasped for breath, seeing only his staring black eyes. More men appeared and crowded me.

The first cop was still speaking. 'Her body was found on land, near your home, her clothes and property were in your house. Yes, we've been there to search,' he smirked.

The terror loosened my tongue. 'You ask Detective Josh Kareukie what happened to Lucy, he and his friends know. I had nothing to do with it...', my voice trailed off. Oh no, they couldn't question Josh now.

The others were putting handcuffs on me when he spoke again. 'You can ask him yourself; he's meeting us here tonight.' He glanced at his watch, 'I don't know what's delayed him.'

Shot in the Dark

Brigadier Curtis Gibbs, woke on the first ring of the phone, snapped on the bedside light and lifted the receiver. He hadn't been disturbed at night since he left the service.

'Is that Brigadier Gibbs,' a soft Welsh accent.

'It is. Who is this?' he demanded.

'It's about your wife.'

Curtis felt the blood drain from his face and his hands tingle.

He'd feared that the call was about Heloise, who had left to take the midnight flight to Hong Kong. He frowned, the clock showed 4am, she should still be in mid-flight.

His agile mind flitted over the possibilities; sickness, car crash, plane crash.

'What's happened, who's speaking?' He asked sharply.

'Doesn't matter,' the Welshman said calmly.

'Yes. Yes man, what has happened?'

'Well, Curtis, your wife Heloise left home last night and drove to Heathrow, to take a flight to Hong Kong.'

'That's correct,' Curtis snapped.

'Only partly,' the man said softly, 'She did not take the flight, she's been grounded, so to speak.'

'For Gods' sake, tell me what has happened to her.' Curtis was on his feet now and panting, as he held on to the four poster.

'Heloise will not be going to Hong Kong and will not be going home either, but she's quite safe for the time being.'

'What have you done to her?' he bellowed.

'Shut up and listen to me.' He was unfazed by the military manner.

'If anything happens to her, I'll kill you,' Curtis yelled.

'Carry out my instruction to the letter and she'll be safe. Firstly, don't speak to anyone about this.'

Curtis sighed and raised his eyes to the ceiling. Damn the civvy, but he had to play along, he needed to know more, then he'd make him pay.

'Don't contact the police or any of your army cronies. Slightest move in that direction and you'll never see the beautiful Heloise again.'

Curtis cursed but the man carried on. 'Stay at home and wait until I call. You can sleep, you're going to need it.'

When the line was dead Curtis beat the bed with the handset and cursed out loud. He cradled his cropped head in his hands and took deep breaths. What was the kidnapper after? He hadn't demanded money? Surely that was what this was all about. There had been photographs of their wedding in the papers, the low-life would have worked out that he was well off and would pay for his wife's safety.

He paced the room, then stripped off his pyjamas and dressed in jeans and an army pullover. What if he were a terrorist? What hope would he have of seeing her again even if he complied with their demands?

He opened her wardrobe and ran a hand over the soft material of her dresses. He closed the door when tears welled up. Why us, just when we were settled? This character didn't realise who he was up against. He had contacts in Special Services and MI6, they could trace the caller.

As he tied his boot laces, a thought struck him like a bullet. He'd been upset and forgot. He grabbed the handset and pumped the keys but closed his eyes and sighed, at the news that the caller had withheld their number.

He stomped down the wide stairs and across the tiled hallway to the kitchen where he poured and drank a tumbler of milk. The menace in the man's voice playing over, *don't contact the police or anyone else.* This stranger had known the details of her journey. Who the hell was he? Curtis screwed up his face and clutched the stab of ice in his chest. Losing her to friends in Hong Kong for a few weeks had been bad enough, but this...

He crossed the hall to his study and slumped at the desk. 'Why me, I've always done my best in the most damn awful situations, always been fair. I've always played by the rules.' He had to pay the kidnapper whatever he asked, more than he asked, to get her back safely, and then he'd go after him, teach him not to fuck with an army officer.

In the downstairs cloakroom, he splashed water on his face. Concentrate. Think. The bastard has given you time, to stew on this. Don't play it his way. Don't let him get into your head.

A new thought sent him grabbing for his mobile. Heloise's mobile phone, she may have concealed it from them, at least he'd hear her voice... know that she was alive.

One, two, three, he counted the tones all the way to twelve, then silence... 'Heloise, Heloise, it's Curtis', his voice broke.

Silence.

'Heloise speak to me please.'

'You were told not to contact anyone, Brigadier. You have disobeyed my orders already.'

He shot to his feet on hearing the Welsh accent. 'No, no, I was so concerned about her,' he hated the whine in his voice.

'Listen to me, Gibbs, I said she's safe for now, but you had to break the rules so now I have to punish her.'

'No,' Curtis cried.

'Oh yes, you need a reminder to do as you're bloody well told. I'll cut off her dark locks, you look out for them in your mail.'

Curtis clenched his teeth.

'Now listen to me man. Don't speak to anyone and start working out how quickly you can get £5,000 in cash for this morning. That's for starters, I'll tell you what else I want later.'

'What, how can I...?'

'And don't try to call her again, the mobile's going in the furnace.' The line was cut.

Furnace, his face screwed up, why were they near a furnace? Choking back the bile he dropped into the swivel chair. What had the scum said, get 5,000, and then what...? The police had to be told, not the county force, but the Met. He'd call Keeble in strict confidence; he'd know what to do. Then he remembered her long raven hair, free and flowing to her bare shoulders. He'd kill the animal.

*

The sun cast shadows of the poplars on the lawns as Curtis forced himself to breakfast on porridge and toast, washed down with cups of black coffee. Starving before battle was not for professionals. He had also retrieved his automatic hand gun from the safe in the fake chimney breast, behind the genuine Constable. He eased it down the back of his waist band and stood straight. Uncomfortable but reassuring.

An old tweed jacket lay ready on the sofa, an envelope containing £5,000, also from the safe, protruded from the inside pocket. He had not slept or spoken to his friend Keeble at the Met.

At 7 am when the phone rang, the breakfast surged up to his throat.

'Lovely morning, I've been out already, had to go to the mail box you see.' Said the sing-song voice.

Curtis closed his eyes, the message was clear, he had cropped her hair.

'Now listen to me, and when I've finished you repeat it all back and get it right for your own sake.'

As Curtis listened, his heart beat fast and his strength drained from him. When the man demanded, 'Repeat,' he stammered, 'what is the sense in all this?'

'Repeat, you bastard', he bellowed.

Curtis croaked, 'I am to go into Maidstone and find 'South Coast Autos', a used car dealer in Paradise Street. There's a red Vauxhall Astra on the forecourt with a price tag of £5,000. Give me the registration number again.' As the man spoke, he scribbled it down.

'Go on, now.' He said.

'I buy that car and no other and pay the asking price. Then drive it home, I must get back by 10.30am and wait for your call... Is my wife alright?' He blurted out.

'You've got it,' and the line went dead.

Curtis swung his jacket on, and felt a pang of fear. He realised that he could not use the Jag for the outward journey as he would be driving the Astra on the return trip. He grabbed his mobile and booked a cab. There was plenty of time.

What the hell were they going to make him do with the old banger, a spike turned in his gut. His demands hadn't mentioned money yet, this low life was more sinister than that. A robbery perhaps, the old car could be for a ram raid. If he did it and survived would the law take his circumstances into account? His hands shook. Suppose they were terrorists and wanted to use the car as a bomb. Would he be expected to kill innocent civilians? No, he would not do it. But what about Heloise...?

Keeble's number was in his contacts, he turned it up then froze. The macabre vision of an envelope with a wad of her hair poking from it hit him like a punch in the gut. The scum had touched her, cut her hair while she struggled. He'll kill her, he moaned, pocketing the phone.

His cab turned up and they soon swooped through the lanes. Curtis closed his eyes as nausea swept through him. He swallowed but it wouldn't pass. When they reached the commuter traffic and began to crawl, he felt better. The driver matched his mood and drove in silence, while in his head, Curtis argued his defence from the dock.

He paid the driver and reached under his jacket to adjust the pistol in his waistband before walking down a street of fly posters and graffiti to the premises of 'South Coast Autos'.

The weary vehicles were packed tight on a corner plot in front of a caravan office. Gaudy windscreen stickers showed prices and credit terms. While pretending to check an interior through cupped hands Curtis scanned the office and the leather clad man observing him from the doorway. He shook his head and continued down the line. Where was the bloody Astra?

It was after 9am when he found it, minus a side mirror and with a dented wing. The peeling price tag begged for £5,000.

'Don't you want to try it first,' the salesman asked blowing cigarette smoke into the chilly air.

'No, it's what I want and I'm in a hurry,' Curtis said.

The man didn't move but stood hand in pocket, fag cupped in the other. 'Look mate, are you sure about this.'

'Yes, I am, please hurry.'

'Look here.' The man took his arm and turned him to face where the car stood. 'See how many cars I got to move to get it out. He counted out loud, 'one, two, three and the next row will have to go; four, five, six. That'll be seven lots of keys to find, two clamps to get off and seven cold engines to get started. Now if you're taking the piss then I'm doin a lot of work for nuffink.'

'Look, I want it.' Curtis shouted at the man and received a cold stare. 'I'll pay in cash, right now.' Curtis pulled his arm from the man's grasp. 'Now be quick.'

'You got five grand in cash?' His eyebrows lifted.

Curtis silently displayed the contents of the envelope.

The man nodded with a smirk. 'Come this way sir,' he led him into the office and the smell of sweat and engine oil.

Orders to move the cars were barked to a boy slouched on a plastic chair, eating crisps and clocking a tabloid.

When the boy had gone, the man relieved Curtis of his cash deftly transferring it to his own jacket pocket.

Curtis had considered giving a false name and address for the garage to purchase the car but gave up on the idea in case it should cause more problems with the police later. If he had to commit crime, so be it. A moment later he was thankful he hadn't lied when the man checked his driving licence.

Outside engines revved and the smell of burning oil stung his nostrils. There was no urgency in the boy's movements and Curtis kept watching the seconds tick by on a dusty clock advertising BP Oil.

The man darted about the office and quickly produced a receipted bill of sale and registration documents, 'It's MOTd for a month sir.' He ushered Curtis out and yelled to the boy to get a move on.

At 9.40 he dropped onto the stained material of the driver's seat. Only fifty minutes to the next phone call, even on a quiet day he'd need that to get home.

Cringing at the racket thrown out by the old car, his wild acceleration got him into every gap in the traffic. Gears crashed, smoke blew, and red lights were jumped in his bid to get to his home phone. Throughout, the picture in his minds' eye was of Heloise bound and gagged before a blistering furnace.

It was 10.30 when the Astra slithered to a halt on the gravel drive next to his Jag.

He could hear the house phone warbling as he fumbled with the front door keys, cursing as he charged break-neck into the study in time to hear the last ring.

'Damn, damn you.' It was no surprise to find that the caller had withheld their number.

Slumped in the swivel chair with the gun on his desk, he waited staring at the aberration parked on his drive. What sinister plan did they have for him and Heloise? Resting his head in his hands he groaned out loud.

Each slothful minute pumped pressure inside his head. He was trying to massage the back of his neck when the phone warbled again.

'Can't you carry out a simple instruction? I said be back by 10.30.' He was furious. Curtis's attempts to interrupt were stifled by a torrent of curses. 'Now, for that pathetic performance a privilege will be taken from your wife. She will no longer be allowed to wash.'

'You animal,' Curtis roared.

'Shut up, or I'll cut her bloody finger off. Satisfied?'

Curtis clenched his teeth to hold back the torrents of abuse churning inside.

'Now you listen to me Brigadier. Can you see the car from where you are?'

Curtis stood; he had a sight line through the Georgian window to the dull red of the banger. 'Yes.'

'Firstly, my name is Ian Nickson. Does that mean anything to you?'

Curtis was shocked at this revelation. Why had he revealed his own name.? The man's a maniac. Cold crept to his gut.

'I don't know you,' he murmured.

'I once had a daughter called Leanne Nickson,' Curtis shuddered and dropped into a chair. He couldn't understand what was happening, but he knew the girl's name well.

'That must clear things up a bit for you,' Nickson said crisply.

The horror of the situation sank Curtis's hopes of ever seeing Heloise alive again. 'Wait, I...'

'Shut the fuck up and listen.'

Curtis waited for the girl's father to turn the knife, hope gushing away.

'As you well know my only daughter, the best thing in my miserable life, was murdered by squaddies serving under you, in your bloody army.'

'No,' Curtis wailed, 'it was suicide.'

'Don't you ever say that she committed suicide again or I'll put the phone down and kill your precious bitch,' words like bullets.

Curtis wanted to vindicate himself but clamped his mouth shut.

'She was bullied and sexually harassed by your, so called, soldiers. Then shot by a coward to silence her.' He was shouting now, 'and no one has even been tried for it. There's been no bloody justice.'

Curtis clutched the phone. What could he do? He was sunk, it had all been outside of his control.

'There were others murdered too, boy soldiers and all the killers were under your command and you let the kids die and did nothing, except take a fat sum to retire early.'

'We investigated, every occurrence, there was no evidence,' Curtis wailed.

'There has not been a proper investigation, only you toy soldiers covering up for each other. You claimed that the evidence didn't warrant one. Evidence is what I want to talk about. You explain how a suicide shoots themselves with a rifle...twice. There were two bullets in my girl.'

Curtis could hear the man wheezing. So that was it, Heloise's life for Leanne Nickson's. He'd keep him talking, get the police on his mobile.

'What do you think the car's for?' Nickson's voice stopped him in his attempt to reach for the other phone.

'Maybe for a robbery...,' he held back on the more sinister alternative of a car bomb.

'Shows how much attention you've paid to my daughter's murder,' snarled Nickson. I'll take you through it. She was shot while guarding the perimeter fence, alone, at night. A civilian worker leaving camp was the first to hone in on the shots and he found Leanne. But you're familiar with all this aren't you, Brig?'

'Yes,' Curtis whispered, horrified as to where it was leading.

'Well the civilian saw a red Vauxhall Astra, near the scene. The police have never located the car or its owner who could be a witness or the killer. Neither the police nor the military could locate the car...but I did. Strange that isn't it? How Joe Public can succeed where the so-called fuckin experts, failed.'

Curtis slumped forward.

'Now, with the car and documents in your possession and your influence, the enquiries can continue. You've got access to the car owners name, nothing to stop you now, Brig. Don't think of setting fire to the Astra, I visited 'South Coast Autos' soon after you left, and matey in the leather jacket was happy to give me a copy of the sale documents with your name on, for a lousy twenty quid.'

'So, in return for my wife, you want me to push for an enquiry and hand over the car to the authorities,' Curtis swallowed before going on. 'That could take months even years…what about Heloise?'

'Will you miss her?' There was a curdling chuckle. 'And what if she never comes back, is found with two bullets in her?'

'Please, please, I'll get this opened up for you, I'll contact the authorities, everything. Please don't harm her.'

'You know now, how it feels to lose someone you love,' Nickson's voice cracked. 'If you don't do what I want, you could lose her again at any time. I'm not the only interested party in all this. There were other kids too, remember.'

'I'll do it, I'll do it, just release her please.'

There was a long silence. Curtis wanted to plead for her life. It was an effort to keep stum.

When Nickson spoke, a change had come over him. It was with precise words that he spoke. 'It is now 11.35; your wife will land at Hong Kong airport in approximately 30 minutes.'

Furrows appeared on Curtis's face, too weary to figure out this cruel ploy. 'What? What are you saying?'

'She caught her flight as arranged. I kept you under pressure, so you wouldn't check the passenger list with the airline, and it worked.'

Curtis wasn't ready to allow himself relief. 'But you cut her hair off, and she's there with you by the furnace.'

'Impossible she was in mid-flight.' The curdling chuckle again.

Curtis's thoughts where a cocktail. 'But I telephoned her, and you answered her mobile.'

'Not so clever are you Brig? I followed her to the airport and took it from her table as she drank coffee. Telephone her hotel, she'll be there soon.'

It all fitted, what the man had said, but he had the fools' name. 'I'll get you Nickson, you bastard, I'll inform the police.'

'No, you won't. You think about it. Do you want them to think you are mad? You have no evidence of any of this and I have not broken any laws.'

'You must have,' Curtis yelled.

Nickson went on, 'You think about it and do just as we agreed. Call the police and your bloody army, about the car and the previous owner. Now that you know that you can lose your wife at any time, you won't want to live with the fear that she might not come back one day. He gave a deep sigh. 'But I know my little girl is never coming back.'

Happy Hunting Ground

1840

Crow Dog pulled up his horse at the ranch house and I fell in beside him. We watched as the braves drove a dark smudge of horses through a gap in the corral. The ranch folk had already fled into the night. Our horses stamped the ground and tossed their heads. When I stole a glance at Crow Dog, his pole cat eyes turned on me.

'You listen, "Weak Milk". You're going to loot the ranch house and bring the takings back to the camp. A job like that shouldn't be too much trouble, even for a worm like you.' He'd always made it clear that a fifteen-year-old white boy had no place on his raids. He spat on the ground and bellowed at his horse before galloping off to join the raiders.

Cracks of light leaked around the shutters. The house was a prize for the taking, but I felt cold fingers clutch my heart. I wanted to please Crow Dog but it never worked out, he would find fault again and jeer at me. I often thought of Ma, Pa and my sister, but it was a long time ago, and I had to accept that I couldn't change what had happened. I slunk through the ranch house door.

Inside, chairs, softened with velvet cushions were set around the embers of a fire. The remains of a smoke spilled from a pipe smashed on the hearth. I ignored the warmth and comfort and took a quick look around, then moved on. Someone could be in another room, someone too feeble to flee, but able to shoot a gun.

I called out, 'Anyone there?' Switching from Sioux to easy English, but there was no reply. I ducked through a door into a passage. In the distance, I could hear the braves yelping. I'd get this job finished then join them on the trail.

Ahead a wedge of light flickered from a doorway. Was someone there to need the light? The hairs stood on my arms and neck, but when I took a peep the room was empty. Mixed in with the smell of candle wax there was the scent of women's soap. Inside a bed was covered with a grey blanket, and work clothes hung from a rail. There was nothing for Crow Dog here. I had to move on.

I'd taken a pace to the door.

'I wondered if I would see you again,' a woman's voice.

I leapt, twisted and flattened to the wall, my knife slashing air. I was trapped like a rabbit. My hand shot to my mouth and I bit on the flesh. I waited for her to step through the door and shoot me.

'Don't worry you're safe. I'm not an Indian,' I stammered.

'I'm not worried at all,' she mocked.

She knew the ranch was under attack, so how come she was so confident?

'OK. Where are you?'

'Just here.' She sounded close now.

My eyes darted but I couldn't see her. I tore off my head band and tossed it under the bed. I'd be a white boy when she saw me.

'Where?'

It started with a glow near the door. Like the first strands of dawn. The air around me turned to ice. 'Oh no. no.' I shouted and cowered behind my hands. Through the cracks between my fingers I saw a waterfall of light begin to trickle. Then she laughed: a laugh that was familiar, a laugh that had taunted me many times before. The coldest winter I had known was warmer than that room.

'Stop whingeing, Kit, two years haven't changed you.'

I dropped my hands to see the girl of light. My brain couldn't work it out. I gasped. She was my sister Marnie. What was my past doing in this ranch house?

'Marnie, what happened to you?'

'Welcome to my room, ' she held open her arms.

'What you talkin about? You gone crazy?'

'This is where they brought me, from the carnage of our wagon train.'

It wasn't making sense. I thought my family were all dead, when Chief Grey Owl took me from our wagon. 'What do you mean? Who brought you here?'

'Riders from this ranch. I'd lain in the wreckage, wounded, for hours. Never fully recovered, but managed to live for over a year. I died in that bed.'

So, she was definitely dead and knew it. That was no relief to me, but sort of made it official. Now all I needed to do was get past her, and the hell out of there. Could she stop me and keep me prisoner?

'Look at me,' she demanded.

My hands shook and my toes curled, but I forced myself to look at my sister's ghost.

'How do I look?'

'What?' I concentrated on her shimmering form. Her eyes were wide and her cheek bones high but I knew they weren't bones anymore. Sleek hair poured down to her shoulders. She wore a flowered dress that I hadn't seen before. There wasn't any colour. It was like she was made of moonlight.

'You look good. Just like before...'

'Before ...before I died?' She could still raise a single eyebrow.

'What's it really like?' I croaked.

'What?' she snapped.

'Being like...dead.'

A grating laugh. 'Scared of me, aren't you? Big sister going to eat you up.'

'Sharrup, Marnie. You're not explaining this very well.' I felt my skin tingle all over. I itched to be gone but I straightened up to my full height. I was taller than my older sister now. Seems ghosts don't grow.

'To answer your question about death: you just gotta wait and see. It's headin' your way, too.'

That made me shudder. Did she know something I didn't? Perhaps she could see into the future. I peeled my tongue off the roof of my mouth. Even as a ball of light, she was getting the better of me.

'Time, you did some explainin,' she said, 'like why you're attacking ranches and stealing horses with those savages?'

'They're not savages,' I groaned.

'They killed our folks and me too. They ruined our lives, why are you with them? Oh, and I did see you tear the headband off... Nice feathers.'

'I was saved by one of the Indians who attacked our wagon train. The chief took me back to their camp. Been there ever since.'

She gave a snort, like a horse.

'I had no choice but to get on with them, or die. At first, I thought about escaping, but there isn't a town for hundreds of miles.'

'Look, Kit, the people in this house tried to save my life. I lived with them and they were good to me, and here you are stealing from them, and driving them from their land.'

'Actually, it's not their land.' She didn't argue but chewed her lip somehow. 'You see it was the same for me. The tribe gave me life. I like living with them, and anyway our folks are dead and you're dead too, Marnie.'

Her face twisted and her teeth bared, like a wild cat about to strike. It felt as if I'd cheated her, because our attackers had killed a girl and saved a boy.

'Yes, and you live on, Kit.'

I had to calm her down. She was holding me back, but if I walked out, she could haunt me, or even bring the ranchers back. I took a deep breath, 'How am I gonna help you? '

Her face began to change, like a brush was painting it bit by bit. It became a smile. Then she dropped back onto the bed.

'Sit alongside me, Kit.'

The bed creased under my weight, while Marnie remained steady.

'You can't do anything for me now, but I'll help you to get back to your own folk, and to what you really are. Forget about stealing and dressing up like a savage.'

Her words hurt, all my efforts to succeed as a brave would be wasted. 'Marnie, I have no choice, I am Sioux.'

'Don't be so giddy. How would our folks feel, after protecting us from the attacks, and trying to make a better life for us out here?'

KEN TRACEY

If I didn't stop her, she'd steal my life and send me back east to live with some boring store keeper, or even a preacher. I'd hate it.

'Two years is a long time, and I spent most of it trying to fit in with my brothers, and now I enjoy it. The hunting, fighting, riding, I even have my own horse, he's outside.'

She closed her eyes and turned her face away at the same time. A most annoying habit that she'd had when she was alive. Hell, she wouldn't let me be. Then I thought of something else, something that she should understand.

'I have a wife too.'

Her eyes opened wide, and then wider. I thought her head was going to open like a biscuit tin.

'That's scandalous. You're only fifteen,' her fists clenched.

'It's not at all; everyone marries at my age and has kids. It keeps the tribe big and strong.'

'I can't bear this. You sleeping with the enemy.'

She shrunk and her light began to swirl like fish in water. I shivered and shook. Perhaps I could escape while she was just liquid. But I'd go with nothing, and Crow Dog would beat me.

Then she was back. 'You are gonna head back east, there are towns on the way that you can settle in. You'll be safe with your own kind. I'll guide you and show you the way.'

'What about Mini, my wife.' In the silence that followed, I saw the candle flicker and play my solitary shadow on the wall.

Marnie shrank into a ball of light and hovered above me. Then the ball shot around the room, as if it

82

was hitting the walls and bouncing off. I felt that it would hit me like a cannon ball, if I didn't get out the way. I threw myself to the floor, and closed my eyes. My betrayal of her and the family weighed me down, but as she said, I couldn't help her. My own life had to go on.

Now, she had to go away, because there was no point to what she was doing. I still had to collect the loot. If I scurried back empty handed and blamed a ghost for my failure, then Crow Dog would peg me out to feed the prairie dogs.

'You're a mess, Kit. You gotta straighten out around your own people.'

'Where are you, Marnie?'

When she didn't answer, I rolled on my back and saw she was hovering above me. This was going to drive me crazy. I'd lose my brains if I stayed with her. I scrambled to my feet and she landed in front of me.

'Now you listen up, Kit, this is what you're going to do. You stay here tonight, and rest through tomorrow. There's enough food and supplies. Then tomorrow night, I'll start to guide you to a township. You've got a horse so you'll travel alright.'

What the hell had happened to me? One minute I had a house to loot, but now I was to be controlled by a demon. The thought of staying another hour was bad enough. By tomorrow night I could be dead. Killed by the returning ranchers or Crow Dog. Marnie didn't see it, so I told her about Crow Dog and his hate for me because he thought that I had special powers that only white men had.

'When I'm alone with him, I keep a look out in case he tries to kill me. He's in line to take over when Grey

Owl goes to the Happy Hunting Ground, but he sees me as a threat.'

'Don't be silly, you're too young to be chief, and you're not Sioux anyway.'

'He doesn't know what to make of me, that's enough to worry Crow Dog.'

Lines scribbled across her brow. 'Kit that man is gonna kill you, believe me.'

'Yes, and soon, if I hang around here and wait for you.'

'You wise up and come with me Kit. I can't follow you round for eternity.' She folded her arms.

'I've thought about killing Crow Dog, before he gets me.'

'That doesn't matter because you're not going back,' she shouted. Her face creased up and flames shot from her mouth over me. My arm shielded my face as I backed away. When I clawed at the window shutter, it wouldn't budge. She was a red-hot mist engulfing me. My lungs burnt with each breath. I would die. My sister or whatever she'd turned into was going to burn me alive.

'I'll come; I'll do what you want.' My words tore at my throat and I breathed in the smell of my singeing hair.

'Get outside now,' she ordered, and shot through the board wall without a sound. I scrambled to the bedroom door.

My brain was minced-meat. The thoughts wouldn't hold together. I tried to sort things out in my head. I spoke my plan out loud. 'Get rid of Marnie. Kill Crow Dog, and then work at being a good brave. That's what I want. I'm not going east, just for her'.

There was a bump in the living room ahead, someone was there. I held my breath. I could hear nothing. Perhaps the ranchers had returned and heard me talking to myself. I was trapped in a bottle. Sweat trickled down my back. The noise wasn't Marnie, she couldn't bump into anything.

I froze, hunched, knife in hand. Where the hell was Marnie, she could tell me who was there? Then a voice.

'How long you gonna take, "Weak Milk".'

My knife shook like quicksilver in the dim light. Had he heard me and Marnie? Worse, had he heard me speaking my plan out loud? There was no loot ready, so what would he do?

I took a deep breath, and leapt through the doorway.

Crow Dog was crouched by the dying fire, a knife in one hand, a tomahawk in the other. His eyes nailed me.

'Where's the white friend you were talking to?'

The hand clutching the tomahawk shot above his head and I saw the blade curl toward me...

It hit my head, side on and I fell.

The next I knew my head was banging on the floor, and I could see lightning flashes.

'Where is your white friend hiding?' Crow Dog was astride me.

I threw blows to his face and body, but most missed and those that did hit him, were lost on muscle. He tightened his grip on my throat until my head whistled. I rocked from side to side to throw him off, but couldn't shift him. Then his grip loosened for a second and I spluttered and punched and yelled out, 'Marnie, help me."

'You're all alone, "Weak Milk",' Crow Dog sneered.

The room and my strength, all slipped away. Then I started to shake. The air around us had turned to ice.

He must have noticed and turned to look over his shoulder. I aimed the heel of my hand at his jaw, and put every bit of strength left into it. This time he fell back.

My eyes cleared but I was still gasping. Then I saw what was behind him. With my hands over my head, I rolled and rolled across the floor, burbling.

The King of Serpents arched over us, its scaled body as wide as a man. Its eyes flashed and its tongue licked.

'No, no,' I screeched.

Crow Dog was on his knees and had begun to chant and wail. The serpent went for him. I didn't wait but scrambled to the door.

'Where you going you fool.' It was Marnie, 'you called me and now you're running away.'

The serpent's head cascaded inwards and then the whole body foamed and seethed. I cowered behind a chair, and as I watched the whole mess began to reform, until Marnie stood there, a scowl etched on her face.

*

Crow Dog didn't speak on the ride back. He trailed behind me, drooped over his horse's neck.

Now, in camp, when our paths cross, he just nods at me and passes by. Others have told me, that he says he always knew that I had the powers to summon the spirits. Well, if that keeps the peace between us, then so be it. Fact is I haven't seen Marnie since we left the ranch house. I really do hope that she has found her way to the Happy Hunting Ground.

An Inspector Calls

His boots left ribbed prints in the slurry of mud and mortar at the site entrance. A cement mixer churned while a youth stood mesmerised by the revolving drum. Beyond him men, visible from their waists up, lifted and laid bricks to the foundations of the new hall.

Greg walked through the churchyard, the headstones were topped with frost and bowed with time. He reached the site office; it's roof shiny black now the sun had melted the frost. He scraped his boots on a metal grid before going in.

Dappled sunlight from a line of windows fell on a long bench. The tang of cold air and sour milk caught his nostrils. He found the milk carton alongside the electric kettle, sniffed and reached outside the door to pour the remains into the mud. The site manager was on a long errand, as ordered by Greg, who needed the place to himself.

After switching on the heater, he stood before the bench and stared through the murky windows. He still didn't know how he would proceed? Would the Inspector ask him, or would Greg have to open up first? He found no answer and there were still ten long minutes to wait.

It had been awkward talking about it in the office. Damn them, they were despicable. 'Don't come back if you haven't got him on our side,' the Director had threatened. He wished the appointment to be broken, and to enjoy the freedom of a cancellation.

His eyes felt dry, sleep had not been kind and only took him at dawn. With it came a dream that alarmed him, but no memory remained after waking.

It was so close to the time now; he knew that there would be no reprieve and he'd have to see it through. What if they had read Tom Knight all wrong? Did any of the team have hard evidence against the man? Greg had heard the rumours of his greed like the rest of them, but it was himself who had the problem. Would the director who gave the orders, stand by him if Knight became all moral and complained about him? And what if Gregg failed? Would he be jettisoned with a cardboard box of possessions and an insipid reference? 'I wish this was over,' he whispered.

He toyed with a thought from the wakeful hours. The Company weren't trying to skimp the job. This whole incident had come about because, it was said that Tom Knight could be an awkward customer, if he didn't get a bung. So logically it was just like giving someone a bottle of scotch at Christmas. No favours expected, just a sweetener. This slant on it eased Greg's mind as he sat down on a high stool waiting.

There was a movement beyond the windows. A robin had settled on a frosted hedge, its scarlet front faced Greg. He took in its sleek lines and sighed. Its simple life appealed to him. The robin took off, its movement left the branches bobbing and shedding frost. The cause of its flight came from the gate where a figure in a navy parka and brown trilby was now striding in.

Boots scraped on the grid and the door swung open. Tom Knight stamped his feet and stepped inside closing the door before he looked up. He brought with him the whiff of cigarette smoke and the appearance of a comic strip newspaper reporter.

Greg's hands were in his pockets, one unconsciously wrapped around the wad of banknotes.

'Hello Tom, it's been a while.'

Tom stared. 'It's you.' He paused mouth slightly open. 'I didn't know that you were with this company, Greg.'

'Left the old job a year ago. Better opportunities and all that.' Greg smiled and stood up. 'How are you getting on?'

'Oh, I'm doing the same old stuff. I've been with the Council twenty years now. It suits me at my age.'

Profitable too, thought Greg.

The older man moved in and stood straight backed in front of the heater.

Tom asked Greg about his new company; were they busy and what sort of work they did? His voice was high and he spoke quickly.

Greg knew that these were questions that Knight knew the answers to. This must be small talk before they got down to the business.

Tom moved over to stand by Greg, head bent over the drawings on the bench. Sweat stained the band of his trilby.

'Not a lot of drainage is there?' he said.

'Well, a church hall is only a small job,' Greg answered.

'Let's get out there and take a look around then.'

Outside Greg's breath billowed as he described to Tom the extent of the Works. The older man listened; his eyes focused in the distance, never turning to Greg.

'So, you've started the drainage,' Tom had stopped by an open trench. Below a plastic drain nestled on gravel running from the new building to the site boundary.

'The runs are complete, ready for testing when you are ready, Tom.' Greg watched for his reaction, but he didn't respond to the invitation.

'Some pipes must be under the entrance road and car park.'

So obvious that it didn't deserve a comment, thought Greg. 'Yes, of course, they take the water from the road gullies.' Was he leading up to be difficult about something?

'Well, make sure they are well covered in shingle,' he replied. Why is he stating the bloody obvious, thought Greg? 'Yes, of course. Anything you want just tell me.' He'd emphasised the word 'anything.' Surely that was an invitation for Tom to bite.

'Just do the job in accordance with the specification, son,' he looked away.

The grinding of the mixer and the tapping of trowels were the only sounds as Tom turned and ploughed away through the mud. Greg shook his head and followed; creases had appeared on his forehead. He caught up and they walked together.

When they returned to the site entrance Tom stopped and turned to face Greg. This is it he thought and fingered the bank notes again.

'I won't come back for the drain testing. I'll trust you to get it right. Or else.' He grinned and raised his fist to Greg, like his father might.

'You can trust us, Tom,' Greg said weakly.

Tom pulled up the collar of his coat. 'OK, I'll leave you to it.' He raised a hand and walked toward the gate.

Greg watched him go, his mouth open. His problem had gone but he was floating. What had just happened? Why had Tom Knight walked away from an opportunity to make a few quid?

He felt no relief, only a tingle of fear, the Director would have expected him to push it. Offer the money openly.

His feet were heavy as he traipsed back through the mud. The only explanation was that Tom knew him and thought that he wouldn't get involved in anything crooked. The Director wouldn't admire Greg for that. He'd have to dress up his failure.

He hated them for the way they worked. Nothing mattered but the bloody profit. His thoughts nagged him. He considered himself honest, but how honest was he really? He knew only too well, that if things had gone differently, he would have bribed the Inspector, and that made him despicable too.

Still not sure how he would explain it, he left the site office. Above him the church spire soared to the blue sky. Then a smile lit his face and he changed direction and walked to the church entrance. His pace quickened. The ancient carved door was heavy to his push. Inside he smelt wood polish and candle wax. It was easy to find what he was looking for. He shoved the wad of bank notes through the slot in the collection box. Then stood straight and nodded to the altar. No one else need know he hadn't done their dirty work.

The Last Game of Basketball

The most dangerous man in the world was hovering above me in a black helicopter. I sweltered on the helipad next to his house and watched four choppers performing a dragonfly's ritual as they descended. It was designed to conceal the one carrying the President, from anyone with a cause and a missile launcher.

I gulped the sea air to quell the nausea I felt. This man was evil and now I had to hand over the completed project to him. Then what would happen to me?

They were coming in. I tried my luck by guessing the Boss was in chopper two, now landing alongside chopper one, while the other pair lacerated the air above.

The doors opened and a glut of suits and army fatigues ducked out and ran clear. My isolation was over, but the big man hadn't appeared. Then I saw his Aide break from the group, he'd spotted me, alone on the side lines, and strode over extending both hands. Black hair, specs. and a smile, we shook. His practised courtesy unnerved me.

'Looking forward to the game?' It was a reminder that the official purpose of the visit was for the President to chill for twenty-four hours between appointments. Only a select few knew about his secret fall-out shelter.

'Sure,' I murmured.

A group of civilians ducked and ran from the second pair of choppers, now on the ground. The caterers and staff that would amuse the hedonist during his stay.

Then I saw him, limping across the pad toward us surrounded by the suits. My luck wasn't good, I'd failed to guess the right craft he'd flown in.

The Aide stepped back, then the President was in my face. Burly and sweating in the black suit of thuggery. He gave me a 'head to toes' and exhaled at the sight of my trousers. He preferred the women in his employ to wear skirts.

'Good to see you again.' I forced a smile as he shook my hands.

'Time to relax, you have worked well.' The flunkies forming an arc behind him stared ahead with no clue as to what he was talking about. 'This afternoon we will watch basketball, two good teams are here with us, and then dinner this evening.' His smile was wide. Did he really think that a woman in her forties shared his passion for basketball? He turned away as a dune buggy drew up to take him the short distance to the house. The flunkies teemed around the vehicle like roaches, and kept up with it all the way.

*

I was relaxing on my bed when his Secretary summoned me to the President's office. The door closed behind me. The hushed room dripped with chandeliers, dimmed by window blinds and blurry with cigarette smoke.

He was slouched at a desk the size of the helipad; the suit jacket had gone, and his shirt collar strained at the neck. The Aide standing at his side beckoned. I hiked across the cream carpet and stood before them. I controlled my breathing and thought of the schoolgirls that they rounded up and served up to him at his mansion. He raised his lion's head. I shifted from foot to foot

One hand swotted the Aide away. Another swot and I took the chair opposite the President.

'Update me,' his eyelids hung part closed, as if to keep out the smoke.

'I have spent a lot of time checking that the contractor has dealt with the defects that I listed.' I said in a voice too squeaky. 'I can now report that they are all done.' I was terrified that he was so paranoid about keeping his bolt hole secret that he would have me eliminated once it was completed.

'Make sure, check again. I don't have time to waste. This project has to be ready right now.' I jumped as he thumped the table with his fist.

'Yes, sir.' I croaked, but he talked over me.

'I've been tutored by the technicians on how to operate the equipment. This is crucial for me to oversee a nuclear war from here.' His expression was like someone expecting an argument.

I was plunged into iced water. I'd heard about the pissing contest he was having with an idiot president on the other side of the world, but this was real, I'd never heard another human being speak positively of a nuclear war.

'The library has all the operating and maintenance manuals for everything, down to the TV and the water cooler.' I stammered.

'Good. If all goes well tomorrow, you will be rewarded.'

I clutched at my knees. He sounded menacing, but even worse, a smile seeped onto his face. The stories of his cruelty to women were never far from my thoughts.

I'd tried hard to forget them, but I could see that I would be confronted sooner or later. I was due to ship out with the suits on a chopper the next day. When we landed at an air force base, I would be a captive, I knew too much about his bolt-hole. I still had not worked out a plan to escape.

He was drawing on his cigarette and looking somewhere behind me. The window blind rattled in the breeze.

I cleared my throat. 'Yes, everything is ready for you to inspect.' He dismissed me with a flick of the hand. As I closed the door, I heard him giggle with his Aide.

*

The parade ground had been prepared for basketball. A canopy shaded chairs for the spectators, another protected tables where a buffet was being served by staff in red uniforms. The canopies ballooned and the breeze carried light chatter, like that of children on a school outing.

The crowd was silenced when a black slick of men trickled down the rear steps of the house and across the parade ground toward us.

Those gathered stood until the slick broke up and members took their seats. The President plonked down in a sturdy armchair. Nearby I nestled back and tried to vanish.

The President barked an order to his Aide who turned and repeated it to a wide-eyed chef. He'd ordered enough food for a whole basketball team. Sweet potatoes, pancakes, pears, ribs and caviar. I felt sick.

The President meanwhile took out a pencil and proceeded to sketch on a pad in front of him, oblivious to the players arranging themselves in a pattern around the court. His pencil stroked the page, I guessed it would be another portrait of a star basketball player, probably his obsession, Michael Jordon.

I needed to eat and get out; it was hard to relax and look like it. My thoughts churned over the project and the fear that I'd overlooked some detail that would cause him anger. There would only be the two of us, if he found a problem, what would he do to me?

The bounce of ball on court brought me back to the sultry field. One of the players was dribbling, close to the basket, then he jumped and performed an impressive slam-dunk. His team mates howled their approval. The watchers stood and clapped as if they loved the game. The President had stopped sketching to watch, but I couldn't tell if he was enjoying it or not. His expression gave nothing away.

For nourishment I ate sweet potatoes and noodles from the buffet. They did the trick and filled my aching stomach. Most of the spectators had carried their food back to their seats to eat, leaving me at the buffet table. I couldn't waste any more time on basketball and pretence. I had to eat up and take a last look at the job.

I moved to the edge of the field and slipped on my shades. And walked the worn tracks through the undergrowth. I soon ducked out of sight and set off in the direction of the coast and the project.

I had to walk the whole way. The last job the builders did was to form spoil heaps to block access for any vehicle bigger than the dune buggy.

I needed water and a hat, but would have to wait until I got there. The stores were stocked with a year's supply of everything, so I would soon be comfortable. Small birds flew in squadrons, skimming the ground and sea gulls yelped. A beautiful day but sullied by thoughts of abuse and death. My knowledge of his secret place haunted me; did I have any chance of surviving? Another day and I would know.

I plodded on. I had only one slim chance and that was to conceal myself after the inspection and hide until the choppers left. I might have a better chance marooned on the island, then what? My thoughts crashed round and round inside my head.

As I drew close to my work, it did not tower above me, there was no magnificent edifice bathed in sunshine. Like most of my engineering jobs it was buried out of sight. Like the metro lines, tunnels and pipelines I'd worked on, and now, a presidential fall-out shelter. The only sign of its existence was the bare ground above it, and that would soon be covered by vegetation, hiding the entrance hatch that stood just thirty centimetres above ground.

I headed straight for it. Averting my eyes from the large mound of earth, off-site to my right. The fate of the work crews lived in my nightmares, and was the reason for my excessive prescription drug taking.

As I rushed, I kicked up earth over the legs of my trousers. I had to see this through and then escape. I did not want to join the workers under that mound.

The hydraulics hissed and the hatch lifted at my signal. I was soon down the steps, built easy for the bulky man. I paused at the bottom and sighed deeply when the lights came on automatically and the air conditioning began to hum. Things were working as they should. I kicked off my boots and walked barefoot to a faucet down the corridor, my way lit by automatic lighting. While I sipped iced water from a glass, I spread out on a leather couch and soaked up the chill air. The shelter was a triumph for me, quite a technical marvel. I let the sense of satisfaction glow inside me, but soon the pangs of fear were back. Would I live to put this job on my CV? My inner voice screamed- *be practical, at best you'll be raped, at worst murdered.*

Next, I checked the President's suite with its nauseating king size bed. The smart TV and drinks refrigerator were working. There was no austerity here, it measured up to a six-star hotel. He, and any guests may be incarcerated for a long time.

When I moved on to the well-stocked medical centre, I spotted packs of *Ativan* on the shelves. I used the drug for my depression, a consequence of working for the President. At least I could get supplies if I ran out.

Over the next hour; I checked, cleaned and dusted every piece of equipment again, then I awarded myself some TV time in the communications room. It gleamed and flashed like the Star Ship Enterprise. The news channel appeared on the screen. Situation normal; the Europeans were squabbling with each other and an idiot the other side of the world was threatening to use his red button. I wondered why they couldn't stack their egos and enjoy their riches?

I switched off but looking at the black screen started me wishing that he would be assassinated before he could harm me. All round the world people hated him, surely someone... My plan of ducking the flight back was all I had. As a diversion I got to work re-checking that the operating manuals were all in order. I felt safe locked in the underground pod, and was reluctant to face reality again, but I finally had to climb the stairs and open the hatch.

*

That night, I slept for an hour, then lay awake punching the pillow and pondering the best way to kill him. Perhaps I could destroy his medication. Would his diabetes kill him? How long would it take? The hours flitted by like minutes, and then I moved on and thought of my own survival. To abscond on the Island or to take my chances on a military base. Hours of thought on my lose-lose situation kept me awake till dawn.

The sun was streaming in when I laced on my working boots and a pair of defiant trousers. After a quick breakfast of pancakes and tea, I set off for the shelter. The air was cool and there was a sea mist. My boots were soon damp with dew. Hares bolted from the undergrowth ahead of me. What a wonderful place it had been to work. And what a problem the President's secret had given me.

I opened the hatch and paused, to take a breath of air. Then I heard the moan of an engine and the buggy came into the clearing topped with its mountain of flesh.

He stopped close. I forced a smile.

Before he could speak, a loud bleeping came from the hatch. I was startled and saw bright lights flash inside. More bleeps were coming from the President's suit as he struggled off the buggy.

'Inside quick.' He limped ahead of me like an Olympian jelly, and tugged the source of the signal from his pocket. I had to wait until he was down the steps.

When I scrambled in, He yelled into a handset, 'What's going on?'

'Seal the door,' he ordered, before he had an answer.

I pushed the button and the thick circular hatch settled on the air proof seals. When I spun the locking wheel, I was choking back tears. We were under attack. But why, and by whom?

When I turned, he had silenced the bleeping and turned off the flashing lights.

'Our country is being attacked. I've given orders to retaliate.' He smirked and rubbed his hands together.

'All done without a red button,' was all I said. Then his words sunk in. My family, friends, everyone would be dead. The nightmare churned inside me. If the nuclear fallout engulfed the area. I would remain locked in with this pig for the duration. I swallowed and tried not to vomit.

The President pushed past me into the interior. Was this the end of civilization? How many people in the world would have the luxury of a fallout shelter? Not many, and certainly few good people; only world leaders and the idle rich...What a party the future was going to be. Perhaps I would open the door and walk out into the toxic mists. Perhaps that would be my escape.

'Come through,' I heard him growl.

I forced one foot before the other. He was sitting at a table large enough for twelve. I wished there were ten other people to talk with. A bottle of wine and two glasses stood in front of him.

'The military have their orders; we have planned extensively for this violation. So, there is not a lot for me to do just now. We must wait.'

I was thinking ahead, of when the contamination cleared, and we emerged on this little Island. It was far from the large cities so we may survive and start again. Of all the people to be marooned with... The next generation of the human race could be spawned by an engineer and a psychopath. I didn't have the passion left to even scream. Icy thoughts like frozen peas clustered in my brain.

Mechanically I reached for the bottle and filled both glasses.

'Excuse me a moment,' I said.

'We have plenty of time,' his fist encircled the bowl of the glass as he shot me a leer.

At the doorway I paused to smile at him.

I hurried to the pharmacy, glancing back as I went. When I found the Ativan tranquilisers, I shook a handful into my palm, then tipped them into my pocket. I walked back slowly, I had a new plan, with a few glasses of wine, the pills would kill one of us. But I wasn't sure yet which of us it would be.

Neighbourhood Botch

Why wasn't somebody doing something about it? A street full of houses and I was the only one who could hear the shrieks and yells and window-rattling music. The hazy digits on my clock showed three eighteen.

Cars were bumped up on the kerbs and opposite a couple were grinding away against the street lamp, while a panting bull mastiff looked on.

It was just a house warming party and when the Bollens had settled in, life in my bachelor flat would return to normal, I kept telling myself... Not just yet though. A television crashed through their front window and hit the pavement in a shower of glass close to the trembling couple. I did some shaking myself. What now?

Things livened up. Roaring partygoers charged out of the house in pursuit of the TV. The couple now fumbling with their clothes were set on by a man, who slapped the woman, and a woman who kicked and screamed at the man. Both egged on by the crowd.

When two police cars screeched to a halt the party goers joined forces and swamped the advancing cops like a tidal wave. Batons were raised and bodies rolled and kicked on the ground. I got into bed and pulled the covers over my head, thankful that someone else had called the police.

*

It was normal for my waiting room to be full on Monday morning. Prince and Archie, Misty and Ginger have had the weekend to consume a variety of nasty objects and substances. Plus, there are always the mites, growths and running sores that make up my bread and butter.

Taking a few minutes break, I waded through the cat transporters and quaking dogs to watch a glazer hack out the remains of Bollen's window. A lump of a man in an orange track suit, a size too small for him, looked on. Ned Bollen was settling into Windsor Avenue.

I completed morning surgery with only three cat scratches and a bite from a ferocious Jack Russell named Harmony. There was an itching in my own left ear, but I would ignore that as imagination tends to make these things worse.

When Gillian, my receptionist, closed the door behind the last patient, she brought me coffee. She dressed for work like an Ann Summers nurse in white overall and black stockings, and since my divorce I'd got to know that they really were stockings.

Now she sat on the visitor's chair displaying plenty of leg, while I sipped the coffee and recounted the events of Saturday night.

'It's so desperate,' I said, 'they're such a rough lot I don't want to confront them, it'll make them worse.' When I paused, her lashes blinked and she said, 'Never mind, Rod, it should improve now the police are involved.'

'I wish.'

'Anyway, you're moving out of here, this is only a temporary arrangement isn't it?'

I had moved in over the surgery when my marriage broke up. Now the divorce was over and I was skint.

The wits down at the Windsor Arms called me 'Sketchleys.' I'd been cleaned out and couldn't see the day when I could afford to move out. But Gillian thought I was rich. 'When I can afford to move, but that will be a while. So, until then, I have to live here. The guitar and drum sessions over there are bad enough, but they behave like animals too,' I groaned.

'Perhaps you should put them to sleep then,' she quipped, standing up to leave. She wriggled and giggled into her coat and I kissed her full on the lips. She was warm and smelt of flowers and nice things you don't usually get to smell in a vet's surgery. Then she was gone.

Then the blues moved in. How did I get to be in a place like this? I'd worked hard to become a vet and moved to a better part of town. Now it was all gone. All that effort, only to slide down like this. Violated by those knuckle draggers across the street. Why me? I grabbed the phone and called the local council; they put me on hold forcing me to endure ten minutes of the 'Four Seasons'. Their answer to the problem was to place responsibility totally on me...to collect evidence. Evidence of noise... What a 'jobsworth'. When I asked her how she felt about coming down to watch people screwing against the street lamp she rang off.

Who, what, where to now? I'd blown it with officialdom. I walked round and looked out of every window in the place, made more coffee and carried it round to look out of every window again. I fumbled in my pocket and drew out the key to the drugs cabinet.

The bottles stood in lines like cartridges waiting to be fired. One came easy to my hand, the well-worn label, I read again. A shake told me there would be enough. The exact amount would leave even a blob of a man helpless. Coldly, I replaced the bottle and glanced at the window. I had the means, but I still needed the ways. 'Put them to sleep,' Gillian had said, that's all it would be. That's what we do to feral creatures.

All night my brain churned, sometimes there were short bursts of sleep between long bursts of rap music from opposite. Blue lights flashed on my ceiling and broke one cherished period of rest. There were raised voices, but I didn't get up. My plan was to silence those voices. I shivered and stared into the pulsating blueness. They weren't getting away with this.

In the morning my head felt like a Halloween pumpkin complete with bored out eye sockets. Somehow, I got through surgery and opened the front door to let Gillian out. She stopped dead and turned to me open-mouthed. Then I saw the crumpled Toyota parked opposite with the ruins of a caravan hitched to it.

'What an eyesore. There goes the neighbourhood,' she shook her head. 'A few more like them, Rod and you won't be able to give this place away, never mind sell it.'

Her words tore into me. It was hopeless, no one would help, the police just came around, quietened them down and left until next time. The council made out it was my problem. I had to work out how I was going to cross the street, needle them and get back unnoticed and unscathed.

'You should speak to Rocky,' whispered Gillian.

Speaking with her husband, 'Rocky 3', was definitely not an option for obvious reasons. She called him Rocky; I added the three because he'd been inside for GBH three times.

'He'll know someone who'd give them a good slapping for a few quid.'

Later that day the wires in my head connected, there was a flash of brilliance that lifted my mood. Of course. I would be crazy to misuse my professional skills to harm them, besides... I could get caught. A hit-man was a better alternative, but how was a suburban vet going to find one? They wouldn't be on 'Trust a Trader,' and Google would probably turn one up in Moscow. But there was another way. As I got ready, I sang out loud, 'The Times They Are A-Changin'.

At five-o-clock I was in the Windsor Arms sipping a pint and waiting for the chance to have a quiet word with Leroy, the manager. Eventually he stopped by and I spoke in a whisper. He answered me with a solemn nod.

I hurried back home and spent the rest of the evening close to the telephone. The television talked to itself while I listened to the Bollens practice a composition for drunken voices, out of tune guitar and manic drums. The phone didn't ring; several times I checked and listened to the dialling tone. Outside it was raining, it reminded me of the wet Saturday night a few months before when I opened my front door to large man. Rain glistened on his dome head; his jacket collar was turned up.

'I've got a job for you vet, are you on your own?'

'Yes,' I stammered, 'but there is an emergency unit...'

'Can't do,' he interrupted, 'open up and I'll bring him in.'

'It's Saturday night and I'm closed,' but he had already returned to his car for the patient.

I put the fire on and cleared off the ops table. I didn't like this pushy gorilla barging in; I had planned a quiet night in with a DVD and a couple of beers. I consoled myself that the fee would help as the bills for my two homes were piling up.

A shuffling in the hall, then they appeared. The bald man supporting another, head hung down, black suit soaked through and streaked with dirt.

'What the hell. What's wrong with him? I can't get involved with this.'

'Give us a hand,' he growled.

We lay the moaning man on a table designed at most for a Labrador.

I moved into the hall. I'd best call the police before I get in too deep. I could get struck off... lose my livelihood.

The bald man followed me, 'Clean him up, and stitch him up and most important, shut up. I'll pay you well.'

I spent a while with my back to them, fumbling with the instruments, but I had no choice. I set about dealing with what was obviously a knife wound.

'Appreciate what you've done,' he said later from behind the wheel of his Lexus. My patient was sewn up and resting in the back seat. 'If you ever need our help, you'll get it. I mean that, vet.'

'Thanks,' I muttered, wondering what a vet could need from the likes of him.

'You can get us through Leroy in the Windsor Arms, he's a friend of ours.' The car's tyres screeched as they left.

Now I waited in the gloom, hoping that Leroy had passed on my message, but by bedtime he hadn't called. I'd been childish and stupid to think they'd help me. But the thought of being trapped in Windsor Drive scared me. Those Neanderthals had spoilt my life. I faced financial ruin.

*

Day by day the view opposite got worse. A hairy creature had taken to sleeping in the caravan. Then, to the delight of my client's dogs, Bollen's dustbins were overturned and no one bothered to pick up the mess. It spread down the road north and south of the house.

One evening when Rocky's football team were playing at home and Gillian was playing away with me, the phone rang. We left it to the answering machine.

'You wanted to speak to me.' A gravelly voice came out of the machine I bounded from bed and scrabbled for the handset.

'Don't worry about me,' griped Gillian.

'Yes, I do, thanks for calling.' It was not easy to say what I wanted; I hesitated, perhaps I'd got him all wrong.

'What do ya want then,' abrupt now.

Swallowed. Shivered. Gillian stomped around retrieving clothes from the floor.

'You said, if I ever needed help...to let you know'

'Suppose you tell me about it.'

Saying it out loud while standing naked made me feel a wimp, then I blurted it out. He asked for the Bollen's house number, which I passed on.

'Right I've got some business for Mr Hicks at the moment, you'll know him.'

I almost dropped the phone at the mention of the name, 'Hicks'. Hicks was in the big league, a gangster who owned our town.

'I'll get someone on it soon as possible, cost you two hundred quid.'

'Thank you,' the line went dead. What had I done? I could be arrested. Gillian raised her eyebrows. I shivered.

*

A few days later as I waited for my next patient, the familiar face of the voyeur bull mastiff nosed around my surgery door. The hairs stood up on the back of my hands when Ned Bollen shambled in behind his dog. Head like a bag of putty with bloodshot eyes.

I was on my feet stammering something inaudible. Hell, what a mistake speaking to the thugs, they must have told him.

He helped himself to the chair by my desk, as he lowered himself in; it creaked like a ship rubbing the dockside.

'Didn't think I'd need to come over here,' a guttural sound, 'I know a lot about dogs, always had them, he's my fifth.'

The blood gushed in my ears.

'How is he?' Relieved, it was about the dog.

On cue the dog overturned my wastebasket and began to graze on the contents. Bollen was oblivious to the growing mess.

'Stood on something and cut his paw,' he sighed the cyclonic sigh of the overweight.

Probably that crap on the road from your dustbins, I wanted to say.

Gillian assisted while I worked on the dog. Bollen slouched, the only movement being his eyes as they stroked her all over.

Doggy, once cleaned and bandaged raised a leg and peed over the mess he'd made of my waste paper then waggled out with Bollen.

'Not a great communicator,' I said when Gillian returned waving Bollens wrinkled bank notes at me.

'No, but he cares for that dog,' she said.

'He liked you too,' I said with a smirk but I felt uneasy. Why couldn't he be quiet like that all the time and leave me in peace?

Later, alone, I took the money for the hit man from my wallet and turned it over in my hands. It frightened me to think of the evil that they would do, for so little cash.

The Bollens were quiet but I didn't sleep well, I was troubled, agitated and sick. What had I done to the guy? He wasn't the sharpest knife in the drawer and would be happy sleeping in a skip with his dog, but did he deserve the beating I'd ordered? I had doubts, but the flat was all I had. If the neighbourhood was spoilt, I would slip down and down the social ladder. They had to be stopped.

A few days later the cash was still in my wallet.

One afternoon I looked out; the car and caravan had gone, leaving a layer of scum on the road. I had to borrow from the hit man's cash to buy coffee and a frozen lasagne for dinner. That night my head ached from thinking about my guilt. When the house was silent, I telephoned the big man with the dome head.

'Allo,' the gravelly voice.

After a swallow. 'Hi, it's Rod the vet here.'

'OK, what dya want?'

'I've been thinking, you know I asked you to 'have a word' with my neighbours. Well they've been a lot quieter and I think that I was a bit hasty. I don't want them to take a beating, would you mind if we left it? I'll still pay you.'

His cackle was cruel. 'No beating egh? Let me tell you, that once we tell em Mr Hicks is involved, no beating is required. As for that lazy prat Bollen, well we went around the day after you called and talked to him. That's why he's quiet, he didn't suddenly become all sweetness and light, it took a bit of pressure.'

'What, you've done it already? I didn't know but then I wouldn't, would I? You didn't collect the cash...'

'Naw it were too easy. Taking your money would have been like thieving off you and you're a mate of ours.'

A mate of theirs?

'What shall I do with it?' I swallowed.

'It's all sorted out, relax. Use the money to take the girl friend out to dinner, on me.'

'What'? I stammered.

'Don't worry, I won't tell Rocky. As I said, you're a mate of ours, yet.'

Rani's Time

The knife flashed in the failing light as her father chopped up chicken and tossed the pieces into a pot. The more Rani tried to get her words out, the longer it took. She must confront him now before it is too late.

'Dad, I need to talk.' She worried a tress of hair then tucked it behind her ear.

He threw the last of the chicken with the rest, wiped his hands on a towel and faced her.

It had shocked her when her father rubbished her plans to do a degree in literature. She'd tried to live with his demand to forget university and get a job, but for weeks disappointment had clawed at her. So devastating, that she could no longer obey him.

'I'm upset all the time, Dad, I know I'll get good exam results, but I can't be something that I am not.' Her toes curled in her sandals.

'I haven't asked you to do anything; you can choose your own job.' He stuck a thumb in his belt and looked at her, like a farmer at an auction.

'I want to go to university like my friends, do something that would interest me.' The words tumbled out. 'I want to teach; I don't want to finish up working in a shop.'

'So, working in a shop isn't good enough for you.' He flung the towel on the table. The draught fanned her face. 'I tell you my shop has given us everything we have; house, cars, education. I am sorry if it shames you to be the daughter of a shopkeeper', his eyes glistened.

'I'm not ashamed Dad, I'm frightened that if I don't get a degree, I'll finish up doing something that bores me for the rest of my life' She stepped toward him and reached out. He snorted and stepped back.

'Rani, you will only work for a brief time, you are a beautiful young woman and I will find you a husband from a good family. A year or two from now you will be married, with no worries whatsoever about study or money.' His face beamed, like a batsman who'd just made the winning run for India.

Rani's heart sank like a dead ball. Her mouth hung open. I came to talk about university. What's this about an arranged marriage, it's the first I've heard. My life will be finished at eighteen, no travel, nothing. The juices in her stomach froze and coldness spread to her heart.

'What? You must know that's not what I want,' she gasped.

'I am your father; it is what I want for the honour of my family that matters. Not stupid ideas put into your head by the trash at that school.'

Rani's hand clutched her throat, too frightened to cry, she walked stiffly from the room. Part way up the stairs she trembled as knives clattered into the sink.

*

She woke the next morning cold, with smudges under her eyes. Cuddly toys and dolls crowded on a wicker chair beside her bed. She hugged her favourite panda. What boy did he have in mind anyway? It was easy to flick through the faces of his friend's sons, all light-weights and immature. To spend an evening with them would be torment, never mind a lifetime. She stroked the panda and clenched her teeth. If she turned her father's choice down, he'd force her into it. He went into a fit of rage whenever her older brother, Anish contradicted him.

A photograph of her mother stood on her night table; the picture glass was cold when she held it to her lips. 'Why did you have to die?' she moaned. Laid on the bed still clutching the picture, images of sleeping with a man she hated tore at her. It won't happen, she'd have to run away, anything would be better than that. She'd call the Housing Association to see if they could get a flat for her. She hadn't called them since her last argument with her father.

In a quiet study room Rani sobbed out her story to her favourite tutor, Meg Wells. 'He's my father and he doesn't want me. I'm going to leave home and throw everything away, just because of him and his old ways.'

Meg patted her arm. 'Are you sure that he wants to marry you off or is it a threat to make you work harder?'

'No doubt about it. He talks only of honour and money, not about what I want.' A burst of laughter came from the next room.

'You should seriously consider whether you could go along with getting married, before you do anything rash.'

'What? Look Meg, I'm not being forced into a marriage.' She sniffed.

'Couldn't your father be persuaded to change his mind? I mean by the Principal or me.'

'No way, he would go ballistic if he knew I was talking to you about it. The family would gang up on us.'

'If I can't talk to him, then how do you expect me to help you?' Meg sighed.

Icy fingers crept up Rani's spine. She looked sideways at Meg and saw her gaze into space. Where was the indignation, the speech on justice, what had happened to Meg the rebel?

'Meg, I'm scared. A cousin of mine drank bleach to get away from her family's so-called honour. She died, Meg. A young girl bullied to death.' She whispered with a sob.

'You must realise if you leave home, you could burn your bridges with the family. That could mean forever, Rani, especially now your mother has passed on. The men may never forgive you.' Her friend had turned tutor.

'Forever', the word stung her. She wouldn't see her family forever… She visualised her younger brother, Tarun, laughing and larking around. What about her grandparents, aunts, uncles and cousins… Forever?

Meg reached for her hand, as Rani squeezed it tight, she saw Meg glance away. 'Think it through carefully, don't do anything hasty,' she said.

Rani recoiled; she's just like the other tutors, one of us until they must step out of their cosy bubble.

'Meg, I can't talk to anyone about this. I'm terrified that if I don't do what he wants he will…get rid of me.' She was fearful even at a distance.

'It does happen, Meg, you've seen it on the news.'

'I'm sure your family won't harm you'. Meg leant over and wrapped her arms around Rani.

The hug was awkward and didn't sooth, tears flowed.

'You're the only one who knows...if anything happens to me; please tell the police what I said today.'

She felt Meg ease away to arm's length, 'Listen Rani, I'm serious. If you are in danger at any time, you must call me on the mobile and I promise that I'll come straight away. Pete and I would look after you.'

'Can I come now? I am leaving anyway and have nowhere to go.'

Meg sighed. 'Talk nicely to your father. Tell him you are serious about what you want to do, but don't fall out with him. Don't rush this; you'll regret it later.' Rani searched for hope in the older woman's eyes but turned away when she found none.

'I'll talk it over with my Pete. You know he's a college principal, he'll help us.'

'Thanks Meg,' but she felt cold inside.

*

Tarun squirmed onto the settee beside her, she put an arm round him and they watched TV; his breath carried the fruity smell of bubble gum. 'Look, watch this Rani.' She smiled at the six-year-old.

The worst thing of all is to leave you my little brother. I will never see you again and I can't even tell you why. Will you ever understand or will they turn you against me? If only I could stay with you. If only I could shout out loud, 'I am not marrying anyone.' Then carry on living in my home with my family. Just like a normal girl.

He didn't notice when she left the room wiping away her tears.

*

She took three books from her bookshelves. When she held the 'Secret Garden,' the memory of a shopping trip with her mother flooded back. She got on with slipping them into her bag. Only room for three. She spread out the rest to hide the empty spaces. Then she took her makeup from its hiding place and added that to the bag. Her face flushed as she recalled her secret date with a boy from school. She'd enjoyed his company, but he'd got fed up waiting for her next free evening. She would keep all her things at school in her locker.

When she reached the front door, she heard her father's command from the lounge.

'Rani, in here.'

Dropping her bag on the floor she went and stood before him, hands clenched in her pockets.

'I've been thinking. When you've finished school, if you don't want to take a job, you can go and stay with your Uncle and family in India until I have agreed your future here. You want to travel, so this would be good, and you would learn more about our family too.' He looked like a man about to receive an academy award.

Ran's hands shook, and her head bowed. No words came. She nodded at him and left for school.

*

Over a few days, the flow of books outgrew her locker, so she put them in carrier bags with her CDs and caught up with Meg when she drove into the car park one morning.

'Meg, will you look after my things for me?'

Meg took the bags and locked them in the boot of her Beetle, then they walked together toward the entrance. Meg, hadn't asked about her situation.

'Meg!'

'Have you thought anymore about what you're going to do?' Meg didn't look at her.

'No need to, I'm leaving,' Rani sighed. 'I just need somewhere to stay until September, and then I'll kiss this place goodbye, and go to uni.'

'I talked to Pete,' her tone was enough, 'he's worried about you staying with us for any length of time. He likes you,' she said quickly, 'but what will your family do when they find out where you are?'

'No problem. I'm eighteen, legally I can live where I like.'

Meg looked at the ground as they walked, then she coughed. 'He doesn't believe that they'll leave you alone. He's afraid that we will be attacked.'

Rani stamped her foot. Meg had put her nightmare into words, violence from her brother Anish, was a possibility. 'Do you think we are marauding savages? We would just call the police, Meg. Forcing me to marry is illegal anyway.'

Meg exhaled and blew away Rani's confidence.

'You see, Rani, as Pete's a principal it could cause problems at his school.'

It felt like a huge hand had clutched Rani's heart and squeezed the last hope out of her, 'So that's it then, they can ruin my life, as long as Pete keeps his job?'

'Wait, Rani, give it time; see whether your father does what he is threatening. There will be time to leave then.'

'Meg, please listen.' Rani looked around her, satisfied that no one could hear, she went on. 'I'm leaving home right away, tomorrow morning. I'll go early before they wake up.'

A minute passed before Meg answered. 'I can't let you do this alone. I'll pick you up, stay with us for a few days and see where you can go from there.'

'Can you be outside my house at five-o-clock? It'll be light then.'

'I'll be there,' Meg said flatly, 'be careful, Rani.'

Rani took a deep breath and strode into school.

*

She had chosen the clothes that she would take and crammed them into her backpack. She forced the pack into the drawer beneath her bed. *If they catch me packing, they'll know, and I'll be a prisoner in this house until they decide my fate.* With her arms wrapped around herself she curled up; the pounding of her heart cut into her thoughts.

She was awake before her mobile vibrated beneath her pillow. She drew the covers round her and wished for a different day. The day of an eighteen-year-old, at school with friends and a family supporting her through exams. *Why can't we be normal?*

She grabbed her clothes and dressed. 'I'll do it. I'll live. I'll travel.' She pulled out her back-pack, and paused to listen for sounds from the men. Then she wriggled into the straps and leant over the wicker chair to pick up her panda, she forced herself to step through the door.

She ducked into Tarun's room. He was asleep on his back, a smile on his face. A kiss would wake him, so she laid the panda on the pillow beside him and blew a kiss.

By the time she'd crept down stairs it was ten minutes to five. Through the lounge window she saw a news-paper blow across the empty street and flatten on the wall opposite. A snore from upstairs made her turn, could the men be awake? Her toes curled in her trainers and her fists clenched. Still minutes to go.

Footsteps on the street made her look through the window but there was no sign of the car. Surely Meg wouldn't knock. As the steps drew closer Rani shot to the door and tore it open. Her heart twisted in her chest and she stepped back. Anish walked in and closed the door, there was a sneer on his face and stale drink on his breath; he'd been out all night.

'Why are you up so early, little sister?' He'd seen her back pack and the terror in her eyes.

'I'm going on a school trip, just waiting for friends,' she stammered.

'How nice.' He leaned back closing the lounge door, 'and where are they taking you?'

'To the country …to walk.' The lies to his face made her breathe heavily, and her face flush.

'You don't seem very happy about your day out.' He produced a packet of cigarettes and lit one.

'You scared me when you came in, thought you were in bed like everyone else.'

'What's in the backpack?' With the cigarette between his lips he grabbed her and spun her round. 'Big packed lunch for a little sister, or are you feeding the whole class?' He pulled her backwards toward him; she stumbled and fell at his feet.

'Let go of me,' she hissed as Anish tried to unzip her bag.

He's not doing this to me. I hate him. She pushed upward then kicked backwards into his shins. Any minute he'd call out, bring her father down and it would be over. She'd never escape then.

'Last chance, last chance,' she growled then threw herself from side to side. Feet and elbows pummelled into him until she broke his hold and he stumbled and fell. His cigarette arced away from him.

He was on the floor. She grabbed the cigarette from the carpet and held it out as she lunged forward. He was still down as she screwed it into his ear. He screamed, and she grabbed her pack and made for the door.

If he catches me, he'll kill me.

Feet charged down the stairs behind her. A glimpse of her father's pyjamas made her screech and launch out into the street. She heard him bellow.

The air was minty cool as she ran along the pavement but there was no sign of the Beetle. 'Hell, she's not here.' Rani turned then saw the car on the other side further up from the house, but her father and Anish were between them.

'I'm going,' she screamed and ran in the opposite direction to Meg with the men stampeding behind her.

Anish was in the lead as she darted around the corner but soon, he was snorting close behind. A glance back showed him wide-eyed and close. Her legs faltered, forcing her to slow down.

Then she heard the rattle of the Beetle's engine. The horn sounded; Meg was trying to distract Anish. Rani began to whimper as he caught up. Suddenly she dropped to her knees. Anish crashed into her and pain shot up her spine, but he thumped to the pavement.

Somehow, she gained her feet and made for the car door. 'Close the door,' Meg yelled, and the car shuddered backwards away from the men.

'Oh, look Dad's hurt himself.' Her father had his back to the wall and was bent forward, the chase forgotten.

'He's only winded, he'll be all right,' Meg shouted turning the wheel.

At the corner, Meg swung forward again and drove back down Rani's street. 'We've done it;' she yelled and slapped Rani's knee.

They slowed down as they passed the house. Rani frowned and followed Meg's gaze to a small figure standing at the kerb side. Her hand flew to her mouth when she saw Tarun bare-foot in his pyjamas. His young face was screwed up and when he saw Rani, he lifted the panda from beneath his arm and held it up with both hands, Rani turned her tear-stained face to him and waved good-bye.... forever.

Illegal Entry

Nicholas twisted and turned, unable to find a sign or shape to help him understand. He thrashed and groaned until suddenly a rough hand clamped over his mouth and harsh words were hissed at him.

Then the dark and heat of their tomb reminded him he was incarcerated. Beneath him rough boards, and all around the stench of his companions.

'Take it easy, it's nearly time, Nicholas,' Alick withdrew the hand that gagged him.

'Not before time.' Nicholas whispered, grasping the portion of melon thrust into his hands. He bit the flesh of the fruit and slurped down the juice like a thirsty donkey.

When he'd finished, he rose to his feet, bending low. All the men had learnt this from banging their heads on the top of the compartment on the very first day.

He massaged his toes, flexed his legs, rubbed his bare knees and cursed himself for being there.

'Is it dark yet?' he whispered.

'It has been for a while; Theo has had the hatch open once, but he is being cautious.'

'He's right, we don't want to get caught having got this far,' Nicholas sighed; he hankered for the long days outdoors with the physical demands of his work. He could now see the shapes of his companions hunched on the floor of their hiding place. Alick had already stretched out to occupy part of the floor where Nicholas had slept.

He sat massaging arms and legs until Theo removed the hatch and the cool night air rolled over them. Two of their brothers disappeared through the square and into the night. Nicholas crouched and tried to imagine what lay ahead. They needed more food, what would they find?

Fingers snapped and Theo growled at Nicholas and Alick to take their turn of short-lived freedom. 'Get going and move well away from us,' he snarled into Nicholas's ear. 'If they find you, don't lead them back here or I'll kill you myself.'

Nicholas's eyes widened and he was about to speak but swallowed. He hoped that somehow, Theo would not be around to celebrate success with the rest of them.

Satisfied that the locals were not waiting, each man dropped to the ground and scurried into the bush alongside the road. Nicholas held the knife at his belt and counted two hundred paces before he stopped and gulped in the night air. He closed his eyes; the air was tangy with salt and he could hear the fizzle of water on shingle.

Alick caught up and tapped his arm. 'Don't fret Nicholas, soon you will be doing the work you love but now we need to run. Let's meet back here by this dead tree.'

Nicholas memorised the pattern of the skeletal fingers against the sky, before they separated to gorge on solitude.

He chased the swish of the sea as fast as the trees would allow, until he broke cover on a stony beach, breakers crashing in the moonlight.

The breeze made him shiver as he stripped and weighed his clothes down with rocks. The knife was comfortable in his grasp when he hobbled across the stony beach. Close to the water he stabbed it into the sand calculating that he could reach it if he needed to.

The silvery sea numbed his feet and took his breath away as he waited on a strip of sand. A cry left his lips when he launched into the salty cascade. He lashed back to fight the cold with all his strength and propelled himself beyond the breakers to the calm of bottomless sea.

Here he trod water while frequently combing the tree line for the shape of a foreigner.

A long way from the beach, where the swell was high enough to hide the trees, he dived and kneaded water into his hair and beard. The tangled mass felt light around him and he enjoyed the soothing effect.

His pleasure was short lived and too soon he had to strike out for the beach. On the swim back, he paused to rest but the current drew him back. He tried again and soon became tired but forced his arms and legs to thrash on. His toes cramped and the salt water burnt his throat and made him gasp for air. He didn't want to die a fool's death out at sea.

Then rocks tore at his feet and the waves threw him back and forth, driving the breath from him.

On the beach he snatched the knife and hobbled to where his clothes were hidden.

They served to dry him before dressing, and by the time he reached the dead tree he was panting and warm. Alick soon approached down a pathway, and as Nicholas waited a cloud slid over the moon.

'The shadow of death,' Alick raised his face to the clouds.

'Come on,' urged Nicholas, 'time to go.'

As they walked each man looked back frequently.

Alick was excited. 'I ran through the woods and stopped when I saw lights at a farmhouse and there were horses snorting in a stable. People inside passed the windows several times. I wanted to barge in and see what these foreigners are really like. Then a dog charged at me barking, so I had to leave.'

'You shouldn't take chances; they could have seen you. Don't tell Theo, if we're caught, he'll blame you.'

'They were only farmers, probably gorging in front of the fire, the men we face are far more dangerous.'

*

Before midnight all the men had exercised and the hatch was closed, fitting perfectly with the rest of the body-work, undetectable from the outside.

Theo moaned as he doled out rations, incessantly warning them not to make a noise.

Sleep didn't come easily to the men in the dark, they had too much of it and with the excess came hallucinatory dreams, which added to their burdens. They had to look within themselves for entertainment as speech could result in discovery and disaster.

After eating, Nicholas sat upright in his tiny space and recited poetry to himself. Some lines came easily others he strained to remember, repeating the parts he knew, until they prompted the rest. In time his brain became weary and he dozed.

*

Nicholas woke choking for breath, a hand covered his mouth, his arms were pinned to his sides. He drew all his strength and fought his aggressors.

'Hold still young fool, there's someone outside.' His friends released him and he grabbed his water bottle and drank deeply.

There was a jabber of voices outside but the words made no sense. Around him other men scuffled as their colleagues woke them. There would be no chance of escape, they were trapped in a box. What an idiot he had been to try and live this childish dream, now he would never see his family again.

He lay in fear, but instead of the hatch opening, he felt a shudder, the wheels had begun to turn, they were moving. Nicholas held his breath and lay still.

The wheels jarred, then the speed picked up. The shake and shudder were a relief and the men settled down in the compartment. They were finally on their way.

When the vehicle slowed on an incline they were thrown backwards, grunts, gasps and curses came out.

'What next?' he asked himself and lay flat again.

They reached level ground and the wheels turned on.

As soon as they stopped moving the sound of voices grew outside. There were more people now. Most of the men were up on one knee facing the hatch.

Nicholas shielded his eyes expecting the daylight to stream in at any moment.

But hours passed without conversation or nourishment. Until it became quiet outside, then they waited even longer.

His companions were whispering. Bread was passed around, each man tearing off a share. Then there was fruit and a little water.

Nicholas dried his hands on his clothes and withdrew his knife to run the blade across the timber boards. He had already spent time sharpening it but drew comfort from the act.

'At least we'll have some fresh air instead of this stink.' Alick whispered.

'Sooner the better for me, anything's better than this.' Nicholas slid the knife home in his belt.

The man on the other side leant over and cupped his hand to Nicholas's ear. Theo was about to open the hatch.

The men crouched as the hatch was lifted and a rectangle of light took shape. The air was fresh and smelt of grass. Nicholas was startled by the nearby snorting of a horse.

'What would it be like out there.' He put his hand to his chest and felt his heart thumping.

Two men dropped to the ground and Nicholas and Alick moved up to the hatch. Theo handed each man a sword that had been wrapped in hessian to stop the chink of metal.

Nicholas seized his and followed Alick out. They ran through a city square, then narrow streets. Fear of being cut down so close to success drove them on. They had to reach the gates before they were discovered. There were no sentries as the city was no longer under siege. The men were joined by Theo and all tugged frantically at the bolts until the gates swung open to reveal the men crouched outside. Nicholas and the rest of the tiny force were cheered as the jubilant Greek army swept through the gates and invaded Troy.

Home Truths

It was unusual for Mike to hug his sister. He clung to her for a moment, then recoiled.

'Mum's death was so cruel,' Lana croaked. Mike could see the black limo waiting for her. She stepped back; her hair streaked on her forehead. Suddenly she flicked her head. 'Well, where's Suzy?'

He'd prepared his answer and tried to sound as if it was normal to travel without his wife, but his confidence dissolved like ice in a cocktail. 'I'm sorry she couldn't come today; she has a part in a play and needs to run with it.'

'Too busy to come to her mother-in-law's funeral.' She looked as grave as the undertaker by the limo.

'She can't leave the play. If she lets them down, she's finished, and work doesn't come along that often.' He buried his hands in his coat pockets.

'Neither do mother-in-law's funerals.'

Mike watched drops of rain form globules on his shoes.

'Perhaps we'll see her next time one of us gets run down by a joy- rider.' She turned and stomped away.

Mike's shoulders sagged; he wiped a hand over his face, then walked to his car. Damn, why did she have to make this day worse?

He'd had two weeks since the horror of his mother's death, but the funeral service had inflamed his grief. His drive north from London had started early, and now he was too weary to fight with Lana. He drove the familiar streets to his parents' home.

*

The old house simmered with chatter and cigarette smoke, when Mike slipped upstairs to unpack. His old divan seemed smaller, and he was surprised to see his Annie Lennox poster still 'blue tacked' to the inside of the wardrobe door. He stood at the window for a while viewing the familiar back yards through greying nets. A glance at his i-Phone showed that there was still 12 hours before he could go home.

Downstairs his father was perched on a chair, his eyes hazy. Froth veiled the sides of his beer glass.

Mike sat beside him. 'How are you feeling now?'

'As well as I can be, son.' He drank, and Mike watched him wipe the foam from his upper lip. 'Lana will help me through. I'll be all right. Have to be, won't I?'

'You can always call me any time, you know that.'

'But what can you do? You're too far away.'

'I'll come up; help you sort things out.' Mike stopped; his father didn't answer. They stared at each other, neither blinked. Mike looked into his glass. His father was right, what help would he be? He couldn't be in two places at once. They talked about Mike's job, and the work he'd done on his house. His father kept interrupting him with questions. 'That's a big job, must have cost a bit?'

When Mike got his father a fresh beer from the kitchen, he saw Lana with Adam, her latest man, lounged against the white goods, exchanging whispers and laughing. Adam had tattoos, and the sort of features that appear in photographs with a number across the bottom.

Mike's fears of meeting the family had begun to evaporate as the sad occasion swilled toward a more social one. His father talked about buying a season ticket to watch United, and travelling to away games. Then he caught Mike off guard.

'Mike, I'm seventy in September, Lana is organising a get together for my birthday. I expect you to be there and Suzy too.'

'Yes, of course we will.' Mike smiled and took a long swallow of beer. It was impossible to explain that he wouldn't be there. He wanted to say, 'Yes Dad, we'll enjoy the day with you.' It should have been easy, what had happened to his life? He'd have to renege on the promise later.

When an elderly couple interrupted, and engulfed his father with hugs, Mike took the opportunity to duck back into the kitchen. Adam had shed his jacket and taken in several strong ales. As Mike approached, he heard him talking to a group of mourners.

'The killer took them to this farm and tortured them in the barn ...'

Mike closed his eyes. Perhaps Lana had found her soul mate at last. Adam seemed to share her morbid interest in 'true murder' stories.

A heavy nudge in the ribs made Mike splutter. 'All the old folks have gone; I need to get wasted.' Lana hung on his shoulder. Her breath smelt like a bottle bank.

'Come with me.' She tugged him by the arm into the 'true murders' group. Mike's elbow flexed; it would always be weak, a reminder of being beaten with a hockey stick.

'How's your job then, Mike?' Adam greeted him and winked at Lana.

'Good, my promotion came through; I'm a chief inspector now.' He'd only tell them what they already knew.

'Interesting job you've got.' Adam paused. Mike could see he had more to say and hoped it wasn't about murder.

'Do you get involved with any murders?' His tattooed hands crushed a beer can like a junk yard car.

'A few.' Oh no, please get me out of here.

'Well... what sort?'

The urge was strong to say; the sort that put a stop to a life forever, you insensitive twat, but he replied, 'It's often the result of a domestic argument or a robbery gone wrong.' His mind swirled to find a different topic that would interest the dope.

'Have another drink, Mike,' Lana slurred, 'and don't bite your lip, it makes you look evil.'

Mike smiled; it was something she'd often said when they were kids. 'I'm OK, can't be too late, I have to work when I get back tomorrow.'

'Oh dear, so important, aren't you? Have you found Lord Lucan yet?' As the group of shiny faces split with laughter, the blood rushed to Mike's head and his fists clenched. Losers, what is wrong with you?

'Well, I don't live the other side of town like you.' Too late he regretted his words.

'No, it was never good enough for you around here, was it? Get me a drink then, gin and tonic, a stiff one.' She leered at Adam who sniggered back.

Mike splashed a liberal shot into a tall glass and used the tonic sparingly. 'It's on your head,' he mouthed. Perhaps she would pass out and then he could go to bed.

The babble of conversation around them dwindled. Mike handed Lana her drink, and stared at the wall. He noticed that the calendar hadn't been turned for a fortnight. How would Dad manage without Mum?

Adam shifted from foot to foot. 'Have you told Mike about Spain?'

'Gawd no, his missus never leaves London, does she?' Lana cackled.

It was Adam who explained that the family get together, that Mike's father had mentioned, was to be in Spain. Lana would hire a villa and she and Adam, with their motley rabble of kids, and anyone else who could bear it, would holiday there. It was timed to coincide with their father's birthday.

Mike drew in his breath; he'd rather spend a week in a prison cell with a knuckle-dragger. He pulled his tie loose.

The group around them had grown. 'Who's in?' bellowed Adam pumping his arms like pistons. There was a cheer as glasses were raised.

'The villa's got a pool and everything. It'll take Dad's mind off things. You're coming aren't you, Mike?' Lana nodded like a pigeon pecking corn.

'Yes, sounds great.' How could he get out of this? Every question dragged him in deeper. Hell, why couldn't they be normal like other families?

'Suzy will come, wont she?' She held her head on one side.

'Yes, of course, she loves Spain.'

Now she'd given him a problem. He'd have to go along with it otherwise things would turn ugly. Is family life like this for everyone? How do other people survive it?

Lana charged off on a recruiting mission around the flagging mourners.

'Tell Suzy not to forget her bikini,' Adam winked.

He hasn't even met her for God's sake. Mike's anger froze when he had a fleeting image of dark-skinned Suzy in her yellow bikini. The visit had gone wrong; he'd hoped for the opportunity to put past differences to rest and leave on speaking terms. Now it was complicated. He couldn't spend a holiday with them and would call it off when he got home. That would fire Lana up again, but they'd be miles apart then.

It was gone midnight when he spoke to his father to say good bye, because of his early start the next morning. The news that Lana was staying the night spurred him to bed, rather than being left with her. As he moved to the door, she caught his eye.

'When are you going to tell her then?'

'Soon as I get home,' he turned away.

'I know, let's call her now,' she squealed and bounced up and down.

'No, it's too late,' he could hear his heart pushing blood through him.

'Come on, I'll call her if you don't.'

'Leave it Lana, I'll tell her when I'm ready,' he faced her square on, his temples were throbbing.

'You're lying, you're not going to ask her,' her eyes were wide, and she grinned. She was enjoying it. 'Where's my bag? I've got the number.'

Mike wanted to chase after her and shut her up for good, but he turned away and feigned interest in the chairs set out like a doctor's waiting room, the loaded ash trays and dirty glasses. He managed to hold off. She rummaged behind cushions and chairs, then came toward him with the phone at her ear.

Mike wasn't surprised when the call went unanswered. He shrugged, so what?

'She's not bloody answering,' Lana shook the phone and advanced. 'I'll call her tomorrow, when you've gone.' She stirred her cauldron.

Mike had to work hard to steady his breathing. Don't blow up now, only seven hours and he could leave for home.

'If she's in bed she won't hear the phone, Lana, calm down.'

'I suppose not, it's a long way from the hallway to the west wing.' She laughed, and Adam joined in.

'Have you finished the lounge extension yet?' Lana launched a new attack.

'Yes, all finished.' Did she remember everything for her sad games? Mike moved to the door and looked back.

Lana held the gin bottle, then raised it to her lips and drank, as if it were spa water.

*

He couldn't sleep. It had been a long time since he'd been in his old bed. Then there was a thump from the next room, followed by stifled laughter, as Lana and Adam prepared for bed.

Wish I'd stayed in an hotel. He kept phrasing and rephrasing excuses to avoid going to Spain, until his head sizzled. He'd never sleep. Then the bed next door began to creak, so he had to blank out the images, and duck his head beneath the duvet.

*

He fought the tiredness and alcohol, to be showered and packed by seven thirty. Now dressed in uniform, he paused to look at the grey room. There were still a few of his books in the bookcase he'd made at school, and the patterned wallpaper had become unstuck in a few places. His past lay before him and now his mother was in the past. He'd never see her again.

He stopped for breakfast in a service area. Lana had enjoyed annoying him, as always. Her taunts had travelled with him. If he had been stronger and said 'no,' to the holiday, then he would not have brought the problem home with him.

She had remembered the new lounge extension too, he shuddered in the warmth of the cafe.

Outside the sun shone. He caught sight of his reflection in the cafe doors. He looked good in uniform, with shoulders squared he marched on. It was just another problem to deal with. He could do it. He could deal with anything. As he thought about the night he had dealt with Suzy, his eyes narrowed, and he bit his bottom lip.

Beyond the Sea

Kate finished reading the article and tossed the draft to join the clutter on her desk.

That article's trash; I had a free hand but wrote about the 'Axeman of New Orleans,' an old serial killer that most readers have never heard of. It didn't go anywhere. What the hell's happening to me?

She tugged open a drawer and rustled out a bag of doughnuts. Jam oozed, as she bit into the day-old treat. As stale as the Axeman piece. The double page spread with the old mono pics left her empty. Kate wasn't even born when the killer disappeared. Her fingers felt gritty from the sugar as she slurped coffee. Refuelled she wiped her hands on a tissue as an email pinged in.

'Come and see me now, Fran.'

'Oh no'. Kate groaned, slung her bag on her shoulder and made for the back stairs. Her path through the other workstations brought a few smiles and nods but most colleagues just tapped away. By the time, she reached the ground floor she'd found her cigarettes and lighter.

The back-street drizzle formed spots on the cigarette paper. She turned her face up to the strip of grey sky, and let the rain mizzle her face. It was too much to see Fran after only a coffee and two doughnuts, she needed a nicotine shot too.

Fran, the boss and two years her junior; neat hair, smart blouses and suits. The bitch even wore skirts and looked good in them. Another drag and she checked her own attire; T-shirt and baggy trousers covered in dog hairs and now rain, just like her spiky blond mop with black 'high-lights'. She shuddered because of the damp, or was it the prospect of crawling to Fran?

I've got to stay on this magazine, I can do it, I just need a story that will blow Fran away.

She teased dog hairs from her clothes and managed to add cigarette ash. When she stomped into Fran's office, she smelt a mix of an ashtray and laundry basket. Fran's nose twitched as she glanced at her watch.

'Kate, please sit. About your last piece.'

Kate's bag thumped on the floor like a builder's bucket as she dropped into a chair.

'The article on the Axeman was, well...'

In the calculated silence, Kate's eyes narrowed.

'Well, what you've written just doesn't hit the spot. So, I'm going to pull it... We need to talk about the next one.'

Oh no, she wants me out.

Fran's crisp outline appeared in shades of black and blue, and Kate tried to stop her breath from snorting like an expiring bull.

'But Fran...'

'Listen Kate, you move fast and come up with a good piece, and then I'll slot it in.'

'What's the deal, Fran? What do you expect?'

Fran ignored her, 'I want you to move up to date with the mysteries. Stories where people have disappeared, news items that never closed. Just faded away. We need research to get new angles. We don't need to offer our readers solutions; we can give them facts to chew on.' She smiled, or at least showed her teeth.

'OK Fran, I get it, but I don't think the one you are pulling is that bad.'

Fran slid a sheet of A4 across her desk. 'Check these out, the oldest story first, and then progress by date. If one bombs, then move onto the next.'

Kate squinted at the first item; she'd left her specs in the doughnut drawer, 'The Sinking of the Jacqueline.' A motor cruiser had sunk off the coast of Brittany, the crew of five, presumed drowned. Kate remembered the event because someone had turned on the TV in the middle of her thirty-second birthday bash, and the news had tracked across the screen.

'There's more information here.' Fran tossed her a folder. 'The point of interest is that one of the bodies was never washed up, one man is still missing.'

'Nothing mysterious about that.' Kate didn't look up from the file.

'Perhaps there is, perhaps not, you can make it into a story. It's a good one because he'd married into a rich family, reader's love a bit of glitz'. She held up her palms, 'Go, and write a story.'

Kate clutched her bag and the file and was almost at the door when Fran spoke again. 'And remember me to Steve.'

Kate turned and controlled the urge to throw everything she held at Fran's head. 'Thank you, Fran, I will. We must all get together sometime, perhaps when you get a date.'

The bitch wants to steal my man and put me on job seekers. What the hell can I do?

*

The next day Kate landed at her desk, loaded with her bag, a cappuccino to go, a packet of Marlboro and her mobile.

'Forgot to pay the bloody congestion charge yesterday because of Frankenstein's bloody sarcasm.' She dumped everything on the desk and poked at the mobile, her teeth clenched.

'At least you beat her in the man contest,' retorted the girl at the next desk.

'What?' Text done Kate glared at her over the screen.

'I said, at least you've got the satisfaction of winning the man you two were fighting over.'

'Paleese, piss-off. He's my man and that bitch snogged him at the office party, that's all.' She dropped into her chair and took a long suck of caffeine through the cup lid.

And he does nothing more exciting than go to work and walk his bloody hounds. That's why I'm out drinking with you bunch of losers every night. She ran her fingers through her hair and snagged a few knots.

What possessed me to give up my flat for yet another man? I wanna go home, to a real home, not a life style covered in dog hairs. And I want a job without a cow for a boss.

*

Throughout the morning, she flashed between the papers in Fran's file, the Internet and the back alley. She read everything. *The Jacqueline overturned in a storm off Brittany with the loss of all hands, an English couple, the Wilson's, owners of the craft and three male friends. They were on a short break visiting the French ports. The investigators didn't find anything suspicious when the boat was recovered, or on the bodies that washed up. One man, Mike Parker, son-in-law of Sir James Trent, Property tycoon, is missing, his body has not been recovered.*

'Not much of a mystery. How am I going to find out where a guy, who was launched into the channel finished up?' She moaned.

*

Kate's nose twitched; Sir James Trent's serfs had been over-generous with the 'Mr Sheen' on his mahogany desk. Surrey sunbeams pierced the lead light windows behind him.

'Do you think that Mike Parker could have survived? She watched his flint face for signs of a spark. Milliseconds turned into seconds.

'Tell me what you know, young lady, you must have good reason to publish an article on a fairly mundane disaster, now three years old.'

A bloody control freak this one. I'll need to suck up a bit; I can't afford to be kicked out by his flunkies yet.

'I'm going over the old ground, Sir James, to see if there could be another reason for Mike Parkers' disappearance.'

'Isn't drowning a good enough reason for him to disappear?' He stared at her, as if he'd never seen a woman in blue jeans and a tartan jacket, with feral hair, before.

'If nothing drops out, so be it, I can't write the story.' The distant works of a clock began to ratchet up. It chimed three times before Trent spoke again.

'He drowned, I have no reason to believe otherwise and neither has Diana, his poor wife.'

'I don't want to open old wounds, but I need to speak to your daughter too.'

'This is a damn waste of our time you know. I can't give you permission, she can tell you to go to hell herself. You do realise that when we learnt that he had been stealing from the company, we were glad to be rid of him.'

He leant forward, eye to blood-shot eye with her. 'I made it public when I found out during the very next audit. Better to get these things out in the open, for the sake of the company, even if he was supposed to be family.'

Kate had read the story. Thousands had been stolen, Parker, as the accountant had been in an ideal position to cover up. The secret as to where the money was, had, in Sir James's words, 'gone with Parker to the bottom of the sea.'

Or maybe not, now that would make a story.

'That must have been very disappointing for you,' Kate settled back in her chair and worked on her smile.

'You're joking, my girl, biggest shock of my life. My only daughter married that man, the father of my grandson...' His jowls sagged.

'Why would he need the money, he must have been well off here.'

'Many hours we spent on that one,' he briskly tidied papers on his desk. 'The only conclusion we came to was, that he was planning to leave us and Diana too. It's blind justice that he was drowned.'

As she walked to her Mini, she could see Trent, arms folded across his chest behind the criss-crossed windows. 'Thanks for nothing,' she mouthed.

The car swished through the lanes; the window views smeared like impressionist paintings. When a gateway to a field appeared, she slewed in and switched off. Her heartbeat fast and her breath heavy.

Parker could have deliberately left home. Perhaps he had a plan and what's more it worked. A hint of his survival could make my story and save my job.

She opened the window and for the next ten minutes blew smoke in the direction of a grey mare whose long face hung over the gate.

She scratched some questions into her notebook for Diana Parker, the alleged widow of the alleged drowned sailor.

So far, Diana had ignored Kate's voicemails; she tried the number again on her mobile. To Kate's surprise, Diana answered. Kate explained who she was and about the magazine, then asked if Diana would see her while she was in Surrey.

'No, I am not seeing the press after the way they treated Daddy and me when my husband died.'

'I'm not from the newspapers,' Kate tried, but Diana only raised her voice.

'We were avoiding them for weeks. They came on our property taking pictures, and one even relieved himself in our rhododendrons.'

It's got to get better than this. Kate bit her lip.

'How was Mike in the weeks before they set sail?'

Diana didn't answer.

'Was he his normal self?' Kate pushed.

'Nothing unusual, he was looking forward to the sailing, he preferred the company of those roughnecks to mine.'

'It happens,' Kate sighed.

Just like me and Steve, him working every night, me drinking with the sort of people who piss on rhododendrons.

'Must have been a terrible time for you?'

'It was, everyone focused on us. As you'll know, skeletons came out of the cupboard, and then just when I was getting back to normal someone broke in and stole Mike's lovely car.'

'Awful, were you home?'

'No, I was recovering at our place in Madeira.'

'It's a sick society, often happens to people in the news.'

'It's fortunate that Mike wasn't here as it happens, it was his pride and joy, a classic Porsche, not many of them left now.'

Kate clutched her phone and held her breath.

'I'd like to talk with you, Diana, are you free if I pop round now?'

'Listen to me, you pushy bitch.' Kate stiffened. 'I'm getting on to your editor and the police right now. You'll learn to respect us.' The connection broke.

'Damn, damn, damn,' Kate shook the phone. Fran would give her hell for this. A few minutes later she sank back into the cool leather seat.

'What a bloody mess. What a bloody family'.

She closed her eyes and kept them shut even when the mare snorted and galloped away.

The voice of Diana Parker still boomed in Kate's ears, *'it was his pride and joy, a classic Porsche.'*

She straightened up and almost choked. *That's it. Say Mike was so hacked off with snooty knickers and the family, that he sabotaged the boat? Maybe he didn't intend to drown his friends; after all, Diana had said he liked them. He'd planned it to look like only he had drowned, and the plan had gone horribly wrong?*

She reached over and rummaged for a 'Mars' bar from her cache in the glove box. It had melted and moulded to her touch through the wrapper. She left the car and stood by the gate wrestling the mess of chocolate to her mouth. She sighed and closed her eyes as she took in its sweet therapy. The mare had joined her mate at the end of the field.

What if Mike Parker had never been on the boat at all. She gave the chocolate fix credit for this fresh idea. What if he'd spent the holiday with a girlfriend ashore while his shipmates covered up for him? So why did the Jacqueline sink without Mike's interference? It could have been a natural accident; it would be impossible for her to establish that now.

Either way, he could have got clean away with the stolen dosh. He could have gone to live abroad, perhaps in France. Her mind rolled over the conversation with Diana again. Yes, yes, then the man who had everything wanted what money could not buy and came back for his rare classic Porsche.

'Wow, what a story', Kate clapped her hands and drummed her feet up and down on the grass. 'Enough scandal and circumstantial evidence to give our readers something to chew on.' She mimicked Fran's cultured tones

She paused and soaked up the scene before her. The sun was painting the fields the yellow of late afternoon and catching the horse's manes, so they glowed like halos. As Kate watched they nuzzled each other and shook their heads, then they cantered side by side down the golden field toward her. She felt that she had intruded on a private horse moment.

Is there such a thing as a carefree couple? Oh my God, there could be, somewhere in France...

She waved to the horses then turned back to the car, but instead of driving off, she hung her head and tried to control her breathing. *It would be wonderful in France on an evening like this. He's got his money and freedom and even his prize car.*

She lifted her head as sadness began to choke her. She ransacked the glove box for a tissue, blew her nose and wiped her eyes. 'Hell, what if I'm right. Exposing him would be like betraying a soul mate. But I'm a writer...'She took out Fran's list and sobbing, slashed her pen across the page, through the first topic. Then she tore her notes from the book and stuffed them into the door pocket.

Trent, Diana and Fran, the pompous gits are all the same, but Mike Parker has beaten them, and so will I.

'Good luck Mike, wish it was me..., perhaps one day'.

'Fran will never know I sussed this one. She'll be too busy sucking up to Diana and crushing me.' She wiped her eyes again, checked her face in the mirror, sighed and turned on the engine. The time on the clock meant she must hurry; soon the losers would be piling out of the office and into the London bars.

The Catch

The ball was high and headed my way, the players faces swung to face me like curious cats. I took a few steps, the fielders screamed out, but my world was my hands, the Australian sky and the meteor hurtling down on me.

'Don't drop it. Don't bloody drop it,' the inner voice cried. My hands cupped, my heart thumped, then the sun blinded me and the ball crashed into the ground, bounced once and rolled fifteen paces before it stopped.

The Aussies went on to win and I went on the sports pages as the man who missed the catch that cost England the Ashes.

The pictures in the papers showed me with a goofy expression. They hammered me; my former successes were forgotten, they meant nothing, I retired a failure. Damon Hackett, the sports journalist, buried me.

*

All glory is fleeting, according to the Romans, pity that wasn't true about defeat. Each day the papers found a new story on me to tickle their readers.

The advice from Mathew, my agent, was, 'Keep your head down, Rod. Soon some politician's going to be up for sexual harassment, then the tabloids will give you a break.'

As time went by there was a marked improvement in the behaviour of politicians, but Mathew did get back to me.

'I've got an invite to a charity dinner for you, they want a group of sports personalities there to draw the donors in.'

When I'd finished whooping and hugging my wife, Cheryl, I settled at my desk with a mug of Lavazza. I had preparation to do, it would be suicide to brush aside questions from fans. I needed to list the more embarrassing ones and make up humorous answers. The missed catch wasn't going to go away, I had to field it. I'd prepare, rehearse and make sure I kept cool on the night. It would be good to get my picture back in in the papers, for the right reasons.

*

I stood at the back of the hotel lift and watched the other penguins crowd in. There were eight of us when the doors began to close, that tied up with the plate on the wall, until two arms were thrust through the shrinking gap and a huge bearded man elbowed his way in, ignoring the combined intake of breath from the rest of us.

I turned to the mirror on the back wall and inspected my bow. Pushing in at number nine, against the rules, was Damon Hackett, sports writer.

The lift rose and my stomach sank. Had I rehearsed enough for an interrogation from Hackett?

*

When the meal and the speeches were over, our red-faced host announced to the diners that we would be in the bar to chat and sign autographs.

I stood with a group of sports colleagues chatting, sipping wine and signing the odd autograph.

'Look out here comes Hackett.' A footballer called out, then merged into the wall of black suits round the bar.

I turned to take a look and was confronted by Hackett, he looked like a night club bouncer in his DJ, a red handkerchief oozing from the pocket.

'Popular tonight, Rod,' When we shook hands, a heavy gold chain slid from beneath his shirt cuff.

'All for a good cause,' I rallied.

'Well, what's new with you?' An innocent question from anyone else, but in this case, my reply should have been checked by a lawyer.

'Doing after dinner speaking, TV adverts and the like, it's all go. What about you, Damon?'

'I'm good, heading up a project on gambling and match fixing. Researching it now.'

'Never heard of it.' I crossed my arms and swayed left and right to look behind him for my fans.

'A lot of players bet on the game, keeps them interested and they make some dosh,' he stared at me.

I picked up my wine glass from the nearby table. 'You haven't got a drink Damon, it's on the house for the press.'

His eyes narrowed, ignoring my invitation, he said, 'You must have had a bet on the results of matches.'

'Never. Winning is good enough for me.' The wine was drying up my patience.

'How about losing?' he shot back.

'All in a day's work.' My cool veneer was warming up. Before he could answer, I drained my glass and pushed up to the bar for a refill. When I turned back, drink in hand, he blocked my way.

'Tell me about the teams you've played with, you must have something to tell me about players taking things easy or fumbling a catch to give the opposition the advantage.'

I gulped my wine and kept quiet. The inference was plain, I knew he was just shaking the tree, but it made my free hand ball into a fist.

'So, no one in cricket needs extra dosh, is that what you're saying, Rod?'

'Look at me. Do you think that I'm short of money?' I'd raised my voice now. A group of people beside us had turned to listen as they sipped their drinks.

'It does go on in cricket, I'll show you what I've got when I'm ready.' He'd raised his voice too, the group of guests exchanged glances.

'Well, I'm in the game and know nothing about it. So, your article will be a bit short on quotes, won't it?' I stood square in front of him.

Then he gave a deep throated laugh, a sneer slashed his beard. 'Over reacting a bit then, aren't you?'

My hand, complete with wine glass, went like a rocket for his face, I hadn't even told it to. His right paw came up to defend and my wine glass shattered into it. He howled and struck out with his left. It was like being hit by a motorbike. I fell backwards over a table, amidst shrieks and shouts. I was pulled to my feet and dragged off. I got a glance over my shoulder and saw Hackett swabbing his hand with a red handkerchief.

The next day he wrote on our meeting with pictures showing a hefty bandage on his right hand. My picture appeared alongside; I'd made the papers again, but for all the wrong reasons.

*

The after dinner speaking and charity events dried up, and I couldn't have got a game of cricket with the kids in the park.

I called Mathew, 'I haven't seen my sports drink advert on TV for a few weeks. Is something going on?'

'Yes, I meant to tell you, they've pulled it for a short time. Be back before you know it.'

Cheryl organised lunches and bridge evenings with self-conscious friends but after a while my need to be back in the public eye overshadowed everything.

'People need to be reminded that you are about. You should write your autobiography or something.' Cheryl urged.

'By the time I'd finished it, the public would have forgotten me.'

'You must get out there and show yourself, hiding away won't help.' She went into the kitchen to slam doors.

Another day, after an argument, she was breathing heavily behind a taut newspaper. 'Hey Rod, are you listening?' Her tone had changed.

'Go ahead,' I pressed the mute button on Victoria Derbyshire.

'Why don't you go on Strictly Come Dancing?' I squirmed deep into the sofa. Her suggestion that I write my life story suddenly seemed a great idea.

'Jeez, can you really see me prancing around like Ed Balls?' The kitchen units took another slamming.

I'd shrugged off her idea, but a few evenings later, I switched on the TV and up came Mastermind. I settled down and soon I was shouting out the answers. A habit of mine, like shouting insults at the news readers. Then I had a good idea.

I was so enthusiastic I got on to the BBC website that night and started the process. Cheryl said, 'But you don't win any money.'

'Not the point love. We're not skint are we.' I waved at our multi-million-pound home with a forecourt like a German car dealer. 'Going on Mastermind will give me good publicity for a change, and I'll have an interest, and I might even do well. My cred will get a huge lift.'

*

The process ran like a train. Once we got on the rails we shot through the different stages. But at the first meeting, Spike, the guy who was my contact, came up with a surprise.

'Of course, Rod, we won't put you in the main series because of your position.'

Oh hell, did he mean my fighting at functions, or being a failed cricketer. Would I ever leave my past behind?

Spike went on, 'You see, we have a special series called Celebrity Mastermind and that's where I'd like to place you.'

'What?' I sat forward.

'Almost the same format as the regular series but the contestants are all celebs, like yourself, Rod.' I warmed to Spike.

'So, how's it different?'

'Each programme is a contest in itself, at the end the winner gets a trophy and the contestants fees are donated to charity.'

It couldn't have been better, only one programme to do and I'd get publicity from donating as well. I grabbed at the opportunity and Spike guided me through the choice of specialist subjects, they agreed to 'The Career of Sir Ian Botham,' which I knew a lot about already.

Cheryl took to calling me 'The Brain Drain,' but I was pleased that I would soon be back on telly.

*

I walked to the bubble of light, the hushed audience behind me. It was as bad as the walk to the pavilion after being bowled out. I sat down and shuffled in the chair.

'Ten points is the score to beat,' announced the jovial host. Then the questions came at me like balls bowled by Botham.

During the preparations at the studio, I'd been horrified to hear the familiar voice of Damon Hackett. 'We'll be famous if we win Mastermind, won't we?' He threw his big head back and bellowed.

'You're a contestant?' I nearly choked.

'I am and we're going to see whether the pen is mightier than the wine glass, aren't we?' He held up his right hand still shrouded in a woollen glove. There was probably permanent damage but I didn't ask. I felt sick at the thought of him winning the contest.

Now he sat in the shadows with my two other opponents.

I got a few right answers on the run. The fact that I hadn't made a complete balls of it was uplifting. It went on…Then I had to pass on one and my heart nearly stopped. Was this the turning point…?

Then the host was saying, 'You have two passes.' I didn't hear the rest; I wanted my score. '…and you have nine points.' I hurried back to my seat, disappointed at being one point behind the leader, Hackett. I'd have to make it up in the General Knowledge round.

Wriggling toes and deep breathing, I watched a reality TV winner stumble through his General Knowledge questions. Being in second place I would wait through the torment of him and a failed MP in third place until my next turn.

I had to win, there was only one point in it. I couldn't lose to Hackett. More deep breathing didn't help.

'Now, Rod Stone again.' Bloody hell, that was quick. I walked like an android with arthritis back to the chair.

'Rod, you start with nine points and the current score to beat is fifteen.'

I almost missed hearing the first question, I had to calm down. It was just me and his voice, no audience, no cameras and no bloody Hackett.

The interrogation went on, I had no idea of my score. Then the haunting notes of 'Approaching Menace', signalled the end.

'You have two passes blah, blah.'

What's my score? I wanted to yell.

'…and you have twenty points.'

Great, I was in the lead, but Hackett still had a go in hand.

The walk out looked like a stroll in the park for Hackett. His gloved hand swung casually by his side. He sat, and gave a nod to the Quizmaster. 'You start with ten and the score to beat is twenty.'

I wrapped my arms about my chest.

He reached fifteen without a pass or a wrong answer.

Get it wrong, get it wrong urged the inner voice. I've got to beat him, twenty is a good score.

A glare that would cut glass greeted a question on the 'Soaps'. Hackett had to pass. I clenched my hands. Maybe, just maybe I still had a chance. A popular music question stuffed him, when he answered Michael Jackson instead of Donny Osmond.

He got back onto safe ground and did well right up to twenty. The washing machine in my head went on spin so I could hardly hear a thing. Failure was snapping at my ankles. Get it wrong, please.

'Blah blah. You have twenty-one points.' Hackett had won. I covered my mouth. My shoulders dropped and my back bowed, I'd lost again. A gloved hand thrust in my face brought me back. Hackett was shaking hands with the losers and giving jolly congratulations to everyone. He smiled in my face and wriggled away to shake the hands of the other losers.

He stood straight with a wide grin as the host presented him with the glass trophy. The sinister tones of 'Approaching Menace,' cut through my thoughts and lights were going out in the studio, we were off air. A photographer was snapping Hackett holding the trophy. Next, he beckoned to us contestants to stand by Hackett for a picture.

At least I was in second place, I deserved some recognition. I swallowed and stood next to Hackett, the quizmaster and the other contestants gathered round. The photographer crouched and snapped and came close and snapped again and it went on. I was thinking how Hackett's woollen glove would spoil the effect of the sparkling glassware when the ex-MP, spoke to him.

'What have you done to your hand?'

I leaned in close to hear his answer. Was he going to make it worse by telling him it was me? Hackett turned his gloved hand as if to show the man. The trophy shone in his hands, but something was wrong. Suddenly he clutched it to his body.

'No,' I yelled and threw myself to Hackett's feet. My heart thumped, my hands cupped, then the trophy dropped into them. I rolled on my back and held it safely in the air.

With both hands holding the trophy I couldn't get up. The audience erupted into cheers as the quizmaster took it from me. 'Well held sir,' he joked, but it was Hackett's gloved hand that gave me the lift I needed to get back on my feet.

The next day my picture was in the papers under the headline, 'Celebrity Cricketer's Catch of a Lifetime.'

Cartoon Graveyard

'I've met all the members of the band now.' Nathan used both hands to mill pepper onto to his pizza.

James, at the opposite end of the table, almost choked and just avoided spraying a mouthful of wine over the linen.

'You're the last,' Nathan added and picked up his knife and fork.

James couldn't look at him; he bent his head as if fascinated by his pizza. Then he gulped air like he was drowning in his own dining room. His hands tingled; he rested his wrists on the table. What was this man Nathan, talking about? 'So, what did you think of them?' He heard himself say. Not the question he wanted to ask but he needed to think and stop free falling.

Nathan shrugged his broad shoulders. 'They're aging rockers with long hair and heavy metal T-shirts. Faces like a rhino's backside,' he chuckled.

The man was serious. What was he trying to do?

'Who exactly are you referring to?' James tried to find some sense in what he was being told.

'I mean Richard and Lee of course. Gordon and you have worn better.'

While James took a swallow of the Malbec his guest had brought, he studied him over the glass. It was the strangest conversation he had ever had. Why had Gordon foisted this man on him? He was crazy, no doubt about it or...what? James had to fill the silence.

He eyed a point behind Nathan's head. 'Did you notice the picture on the wall?'

The younger man slewed round. 'Wow, I missed that when I came in. You four were four fresh faced dudes back then.'

'It was taken to publicise our first album.' James had to calm down. If he challenged the man, there could be no turning back.

'Where was it taken?' The big man turned back to the table.

'Amsterdam.'

'Ho ho, sex and drugs then?'

'Regrettably,' said James. Nathan was another bloody hedonist. 'Aren't you a bit young for our music?' he said.

'Well, it's not my era; I'm more the *Backstreet Boys*. But I love *Cartoon Graveyard's* classic numbers; Graveyard Sunrise and Suburban Doom. You made great music.'

He could see that Nathan had done his homework; a few minutes with Google would have given him their hits. As he topped up their glasses, the bottle clinked on the rims. He slid a look at his watch, the sooner Gordon joined them, the sooner he'd know what this lunatic was up to.

Gordon had phoned to ask if he would accommodate a friend overnight, he had a job interview in town and was down on his luck.

'Only one night,' Gordon had pleaded.

James was used to having guests, the downside of living alone in a big house. Nathan had arrived in a decent car dressed in a suit; he looked like a footballer in a deodorant advert. But now he'd homed in on the band. *Cartoon Graveyard* had broken up twenty years ago and never been heard of since, so what was his interest?

'I saw your guitar hanging in the hall. Do you still play?' Nathan had parked his knife and fork and started to roll back his cuffs.

'I play with the choir; we have a carol concert at Christmas. Gordon backs me on the piano. He plays the church organ too, you know?'

'I didn't,' Nathan sniggered, 'you two sure got religion. You've even got a vicar's haircut, you know.'

James instinctively patted his white comb-over and glared at Nathan. 'If you'd been there, you'd understand. We toured a lot and sampled all the scary things in life. I was lucky, stayed off the drugs, but it turned the others evil, wrecked them.'

'Wrecked them?'

'You said it yourself, Nathan, they were ravaged by the rock and roll lifestyle.' Nathan had turned dinner into an interrogation. Hurry up Gordon; give me a hand with your curious friend.

'How did it show, this being wrecked?' Nathan fired back.

'Drink and drugs. We were late for gigs, argued with everyone, argued between ourselves and split up. Amen.' James ran a finger around his stiff collar.

'You must have hated them. You're so level headed and moral. Look how they turned out and look at what you have here.'

'I can't look at them I haven't seen them for years. You tell me what you saw when you met them.' It was good to turn the table on the smug bastard.

'They haven't done much, years in the wilderness, rehab and all that. Lately, Richard, has been working on the production side, he still loves the music.'

James knew this was rubbish. It sounded like a script. 'Making a good living, is he?' His sarcasm went un-checked.

'He seems ok. Lee on the other hand is taking life easy. Married for the third time, she's helped him a lot. They've a place in the Lakes; she's not short of money.'

'She will be by the time Lee's finished with her,' James played along. Their plates were empty so he took them to the kitchen and returned with dishes of apple pie and a carton of cream. 'I keep it simple, living on my own,' he remarked.

'Bit different to the past,' Nathan returned.

'I'm happy. It's good to make a difference to people's lives.' He shoved a plate in front of his guest and sat down.

'Are you really content with this life, James?'

'It was what I needed after mixing with the dregs of humanity and fighting with the band.'

'You split on bad terms then?'

James shoved him the carton of cream and withdrew his hand quickly. He could hardly eat. 'Enough talk about me. What time is your interview tomorrow?'

'Not until ten-o-clock,' Nathan zig zagged cream on his pie.

'What is the job, you didn't say?' his voice quivered.

'It's for marketing director with one of the renewable energy companies. You know, it's the new rock and roll.'

James tapped his chest to help the food down. 'If it is rock and roll you better make sure they don't screw you out of your earnings.'

He asked more questions about the location of the factory and Nathan's plans if he got the job.

Nathan filled the silence that followed. 'You should go to the Lakes and see Lee and his wife. They're a great couple. They'd love to see you.'

As he chewed, James forced his face into what he hoped was an untroubled look. He couldn't eye the clean-cut imposter; he wanted to punch him. Best to wait for Gordon, he'd help out and two against Nathan would be better.

He drained the wine bottle into his guest's glass.

'How about Richard, would he be pleased to see me too?' He smirked as he crossed the room to pull a fresh bottle from the rack.

'Sure, he would. He lives near the studios in London. He'll show you a good time.'

'That's hardly the scene for a respectable clergyman.' James twisted the cap and filled his glass before sitting down.

'Richard would be amazed to see you as a vicar.' Nathan laughed.

He supposed that would be true, however improbable. 'You seem to know a lot about how my old friends think.'

'I've always been interested in the music scene and when Gordon offered to introduce me to *Cartoon Graveyard*...well, I hung on to their every word, got to know them,' he chuckled.

James shot to his feet. 'Are you now telling me that Gordon was with you when you met them?'

'Of course, how else would I meet them?'

James sank back in his chair, hand over his eyes. God help me, what is going on?

'He's never mentioned to me that he'd seen them.' The blood whistled through his ears. What was Gordon doing forcing this con-man onto him and in his own vicarage?

'You alright, James, you look upset?'

'I damn well am upset. I'd expect that Gordon would be here to explain what the hell is going on. I don't believe you, Richard and Lee disappeared; they haven't been seen for years. Damn it, you must read the papers.'

Nathan drummed his fingers on the table, his mouth in a tight line. 'I can't speak for Gordon; I don't know why he kept it from you. As for me, nothing's 'going on'. I'm thankful for the free digs, I need a hand just now and I'm grateful to you and Gordon. So, what's your problem?'

James admonished himself for losing control but he'd had enough of the derisive comments. 'There's a programme I want to watch on television. Let's take the bottle into the lounge and wait for Gordon.'

When Nathan had dropped into an armchair, he placed the bottle within his reach. 'Help yourself.' He said picking up the remote and turning on the news. He sat on the settee and resisted the urge to gulp his wine down. Nathan had stretched out with his head back; he wasn't drinking either.

'No programme then?' Nathan prompted.

James took a deep breath and let it hiss from his lips.

'I thought we were going to watch one of your favourites,' Nathan persisted, 'Midsomer Murders, would suit a vicar.'

James switched the news on. He knew now that he was in trouble. This was no guest starting a career in renewable energy. He'd invited the fox into the hen house. Damn Gordon, why had he gone along with this?

'I watch it sometimes; I like Mrs Barnaby.' He needed time to sort out his next move. He had every right to throw the imposter out, but if Nathan refused to leave, what then? A struggle with the big man could be fatal.

He closed his eyes and prayed for help and strength, and then decided that he could take no more. He prodded the remote button. In the silence, he could hear Nathan's regular breathing. He turned quickly, but Nathan was laid back, mouth open emitting a snore. He turned back to the blank screen and let his head loll back. Might as well wait for Gordon now.

The door chimes made him jump. Nathan made a choking sound and sat up. James was on his feet and at the door.

'Gordon, where have you been?' He heard his own shrill voice. A squat man with grey hair, styled like a vagrant, swaggered in.

'You didn't say a time,' he muttered, 'I can't stay too long.'

'I want a word.' James hissed, but Gordon was already greeting Nathan. He followed and interrupted their banter. 'You said that you can't stay, Gordon. Well OK, but when you go, take your friend with you. He's been acting strangely and spoiling for an argument since he came in. I don't want him staying here.'

'What's your problem, you invited him?' Gordon's attempt at innocence was not convincing.

'Not very charitable, are you?' Nathan followed.

'I did offer him a bed,' James answered Gordon, 'but only for your benefit. He's a stranger to me, but a friend of yours by the sound of it.'

'Sorry if I've upset you, vicar.' Nathan glared at James.

'You know that you've been play acting since you came in here. You haven't met Richard and Lee. You're lying. Leave now both of you, and I need to talk with you in the morning, Gordon.'

'What are you talking about,' Nathan snapped.

'I'm talking about that nonsense about Gordon introducing you to, Richard and Lee.'

'It's true,' Gordon blurted.

James couldn't speak; he looked at the pair of then through a blue haze, his fists clenched. Gordon was lying. His friend was part of this conspiracy. Why? Why?

'If it's true, why didn't you tell me that you'd seen Richard and Lee?' He met Gordon's eyes.

'I couldn't because you hated them. You said they'd sided with the devil and should go to hell. I couldn't come back and say; hey I've just spent a weekend with the sinners. You would have made my life a misery and I need the work you give me.'

James stuttered, but no sense came out.

'You're getting mighty upset about the past, vicar. Want to talk about it?' Nathan interrupted, 'Pour us some wine, Gordon.'

James shook, now that Gordon had sided with Nathan; he had both of them to fight.

'Why don't you tell us about the last time you saw them?' Nathan sipped his wine and pouted.

James slumped down between his interrogators. 'It's immaterial to this lark of yours, but I'll tell you. Then you both leave, understand?' No one protested.

'A while after the band split up, the three of us met up at Lee's country house. The plan was to stay a few days and sort our affairs out. I got there and they were larking around in the pool with a group of girls. They were all high. I was cold sober and tried to fit in, but it was soon obvious that no sense would come out of it.'

'Where was I?' asked Gordon.

'You know that better than I do. You didn't turn up.' James carried on, 'The next day I tried again but it was hopeless, so I packed up and left. I have not seen or heard from either of them since. One newspaper claimed they were in a mental home and another that they had joined a cult in America. Strange how you managed to find them.' He turned to Nathan.

'I've got a surprise for you.' Nathan pointed at him.

James wanted to tell him to go to hell, but he caught his breath at this new approach.

'Two surprises in fact,' Nathan milked the moment.

'I can't wait.' He tried to be cool but Nathan's next words crashed into him like a kid on a skateboard.

'You don't remember me then?'

Surely, he'd never met Nathan before. What now?

'I was about ten when you last saw me. I'm Richard's younger brother.'

James twitched and his hand shot to cover his mouth. Nathan smiled.

'It's certainly been a long time,' James stuttered. Acid stung his throat.

'Did you forget me?'

'Never gave you a thought,' James said truthfully.

'OK, we'll have plenty of time to catch up as we drive,' Nathan grinned.

'We won't be catching up. I'm not interested in an imposter who lies about a clean energy job.'

'I said there were two surprises,' Nathan growled, 'the other is that we are all going to meet Richard.'

The shock made James jump to his feet a gurgling sound erupted from his mouth. 'You go and see who you damn well like. But get out of here before the police arrive.' He had to get them out, but he didn't want the police.

'Richard would love to see you; he's only twenty minutes away. He's come up from London so we can all meet up.'

'Tell him I don't like the way he sends his invitations.' James shouted and scrambled to the door.

'Come with us or we'll drag out,' Gordon yelled after him.

Then Nathan's arms locked like steel around him. He tried to elbow him but he couldn't move. He back-healed Nathan and heard a howl. Released from his grip he dashed into the hall and slammed the door behind him. Gordon was yelling for Nathan to get out of his way as James turned the key. He paused to grab his car keys then opened the front door. He dodged back a moment later and grabbed his guitar from the wall.

The sound of the engine firing soon blotted out the bangs and shouts from indoors. As he drove off into the night he sang, his voice no longer shrill. He hadn't told them. He hadn't admitted a thing.

Soon he joined the motorway and laughed out loud as the car took off. At least he had his guitar; where God's work was to be done; they would need music.

He yelled at the windscreen. 'I gave them both a huge dose of LSD and buried them. They deserved to die they were evil.' He opened the window and the blast wrecked his vicar's haircut. Wild eyed and dishevelled he put his foot down and shrieked at the night.

Amigos

As soon as my VW clattered to a halt outside his house, the front door opened and Billy appeared, dressed in his black suit topped with the Mississippi Gambler's tie, like he was going on stage.

'Don't go yet,' he demanded as he got in the car.

'I don't know where we're going anyway,' I took my hands from the wheel.

'This is what we're gonna do.' He turned to look me in the eye, a grin beneath his Beatle fringe.

He was still yapping when I banged my hand on the wheel and shouted, 'No.'

'Wait, listen, I've got it weighed up.'

My hopes of, sea sun and all that, burst into flames as he explained.

'No way, Billy. We can't do that; we'll finish up in 'clink.'

'It's simple. I've watched them all week. It's a big store, big takings, we only need one bag.'

You're the one who needs one bag, I wanted to say.

'How do you know the girls will have cashed up just when you come in the back door?'

'Listen, the last three afternoons they've emptied the tills into bags at five o'clock. One girl strolls round collecting them up and takes them to the office.'

'Come on, Billy, they're not going to let you help yourself.'

'They're young girls, laughing and chatting, they don't give a damn.'

'I don't like it. I could lose my job, never get a reference or anything.' I rested my head on the wheel and closed my eyes until the horn went off and we both nearly jumped through the windscreen.

'Let's forget it. We can go to Spain next year.' *Buenas noches Barcelona,* I thought.

'Do you want me to go on my own and come back with tales of sex and drunkenness to make you cringe?' he said.

'No.' I really wanted to be there. It had been my idea in the first place.

'The beauty of this is that it's simple. It will take them by surprise.' He was wide eyed. Next thing he was laughing and chatting away, like when he did his stage act as the funny man introducing groups.

Suddenly he faced the front and announced, 'Right you just have to drive past the front of the store and look out for me. Leave the passenger door unlocked, it'll save time. I'll get straight in with the cash bag and you drive off. Simple and professional.'

'I can't do it,' I gasped.

'You're a defeatist', he spoke sharply. 'I deserve a bit of help and you're supposed to be my mate. Going on holiday together and all that. Don't let me down now.' He grabbed my arm tight and his dark eyes nailed me. When he let go, he spoke like the teachers used to. 'Come on, it's turned four-o-clock, drive into town, we're on at five, mate.'

The road took us through red brick streets baked by the summer sun. Billy laughed and chatted without a pause. I hardly heard a word he said, I wanted to turn the car round and go home for a normal Saturday night. Watch a bit of telly followed by a few drinks in the pub then dance with a long-legged girl in a short skirt. No hope tonight though.

My mouth was dry, and we were still short of our target when Billy demanded, 'Let me out here, Ray, I'll walk to the store. It'll give you a chance to get through the traffic and to the front doors in time.'

'Are you sure about this?' I griped, as he got out.

'See you in a few minutes,' then he was gone.

That was the worst of it. Alone on a mission that I didn't believe in. What if... It took a lot of grit to drive on, I'm no angel, but if this worked out, I wouldn't take a shilling of the damn money. I'd enjoy the sun, sea and girls with my own hard-earned cash. But what if we got caught with a bag of Saturdays takings from Woolworths in my car? I'd have to say, *this is nothing to do with me. I was just driving past when a mate flagged me down.* It suddenly struck me that I'd made up an alibi. Hell. I couldn't drop pal Billy in the crap.

The line of cars snuck on like the snakes in my stomach. Billy's plan to walk in and grab a bag of dosh was reckless, I had a job that I needed to keep. At least it paid for a thirty quid holiday in Spain and my beaten-up Volkswagen.

I had to pick him up in front of the store, but what if I got there too early and had to wait around, how was I going to park in the busy street, and in full view of Saturday's shoppers? Any one of them could remember the car or me. Now, it began to look more like I'd be late. Would Billy be waiting around with a bag of stolen cash when I got there? Oh my God, if we got away with this, I'd never get involved in thieving again. I wouldn't even nick a bottle of wine from my tight arsed boss.

We moved towards a cross road. The car in front had accelerated away when a cop in a short-sleeved shirt stepped out and pointed at me. His raised hand made it clear I was to stop. Oh no...how had they found out? Had they caught Billy? Had he dropped me in it.? My leg shook as I held the clutch down.

More cops appeared and formed a chain across the junction. I was quaking, hell, this was big, how did they know about us?

Crowds of people buzzed on the street corners, what was going on? My cop was a short distance away, arms crossed, but not reaching for his handcuffs.

'What's going on?' I croaked through the window.

The cop laughed and strolled toward me. 'It's the Beatles. Flown up from London for the premier of their film at the Odeon. Didn't you know?'

Of course, I knew, but pal Billy had blotted out the good things in life.

'Thanks,' I forced a grin.

'Won't keep you long, once they've passed you can move on'.

He walked off to join his mates in the chain. For a better view, I guessed.

I waited, I breathed deeply and closed my eyes. A blond girl in a pink bikini appeared and I smiled at her, but she shook her head and turned away. Damn we'd probably be in clink instead of Lloret del Mar, and I'd been doing well with my Spanish lessons too. Already, I could order two beers and ask the way to the Cathedral.

Suddenly the air was ripped apart as six police motorbikes in two lines cruised across the junction.

I held my breath when a Jaguar appeared and stopped dead centre in front of me. I had the best view in town. I should have been enjoying this.

John Lennon's cheeky grin beamed from the rear window. My pain dulled, I watched spellbound as he wildly shook his mop head to amuse the cheering crowds.

Then the Jag shot forward to be replaced centre junction by another class car. This time a girl with blonde hair sat in the back seat, she glared at me as our eyes met. She looked like I felt. I had to get on, not spend my time in traffic, I'd made other plans.

I'd aged a few years by the time the cops waved me on. I decked the throttle, the car clattered across the junction into the empty street ahead. All this agro because Billy couldn't earn enough dosh to pay for the holiday we'd booked.

Soon the store sign came up on my left. The pavements were packed with shoppers. It was ages since Billy had left me; he must have got through the store by now. It was a long time for him to stand around with a straight face and a bag of stolen cash.

I stopped alongside the entrance and with my teeth clenched and my eyes screwed up, I combed the crowds for a black suit and a Beatle haircut.

Now there were honking horns as drivers struggled to pass me. I continued my search but there was no sign of him. I'd have to move soon, but could I leave a mate to his stupid fate? It would be difficult even for him to talk his way out of this. Then a way ahead I saw a figure, head down, zig zagging through the crowd. I pulled out to a barrage of horn blowing and fist waving. Then I noticed that two or three suits were chasing Billy. The worst had happened, because I'd been late.

A rap on the window nearly stopped my heart. Then the passenger door was dragged open.

'No,' I exclaimed, my foot came off the clutch and the car lurched and stalled.

A round face with bushy eyebrows appeared and grew closer. The car rocked as he dropped into the seat beside me.

'Please follow that chap running', the man was tense, 'he's just stolen a bag of cash from Woolworths. I'm a manager there. Thank you so much for your help.'

No reply came from my numb head. I drove on auto pilot, bursting with thoughts. I couldn't catch my own mate. What was I to do? Perhaps fake a breakdown or run out of petrol? A deliberate crash? I could feign a heart attack; it wasn't far off anyway.

Next time I looked the runner had gone. The Manager sighed, I felt him look at me. Suddenly, a bang on the window nearly emptied my bladder.

'Stop,' shouted the Manager, 'let these two in they work for me.'

'Be my guest,' I murmured as he jumped out and ushered two younger men into the back seat.

'We saw him go down the side street,' one squealed.

'Let's go,' enthused the Manager.

In the mirror my face was as red as a bullfighter's cape.

The shadows of the side street were a relief. There were fewer people and thankfully none of them was Billy. It would be horrific to meet up with him like this. What could I say? *Oh, I've changed sides mate. Didn't really go along with all this.*

At the end of the street I paused for as many seconds as I dared to rack up his lead.

'Left,' the Manager ordered. Then I saw Billy. Slower now and no sign of a cash bag, he must have dumped it. Slightly less suicidal, I drove on. At least they wouldn't catch him with the loot.

He took the next right and we followed.

It would be easy to catch him now, just a short distance to go. A new fear racked my soul. When Billy saw the car, would he think that I'd come to save him? Would he notice my passengers?

The tyres hummed over worn cobbles, there were no shoppers in this old part of town. Warehouses stood black against the low sun. Soon we'd take the lone figure ahead. I thought again about faking a break down. Then the Manager nudged me.

'Get a move on, we've got him.'

'He's run himself out,' chirped one of the young men.

The stutter of my engine at last reached Billy's ears and he flashed a look back, then slowed to a walk, studied nonchalance on his face. At least he'd realised this was no rescue vehicle.

The Manager was barking instructions and grabbing the wheel. 'Turn in front of him. Trap him against the wall.' I swung the nose of the Beetle in front of Billy. The car door swung open, three vigilantes scrabbled out and surrounded him.

What now for me, the accomplice and pursuer? I sank deeper into my seat and stared at the cobbled way ahead.

'What's up?' I heard Billy ask.

'You know what you did,' accused the Manager. 'Where's the money?'

'What are you talking about?' There was a chuckle in Billy's words. The pursuers paused, as if they doubted themselves. Then they all bellowed at once. 'You grabbed a bag of money from the store.' 'We saw you do it.' 'Where's the cash?'

'Hold on you lot, that's a serious accusation,' he faced his audience. When I chanced a look at him between his captors, his breathing was already controlled. He slid a packet of fags from his pocket and lit one from his lighter.

'You're coming back with us,' the Manager wasn't to be fooled.

'Am I hell, you've no authority over me.' Tough words but it was three to one.

'The police have authority, and they've been called.' The Manager was winning.

I tried to see his face through the small crowd, then I caught a flash of pink. The girl in the bikini faced me, blonde and tanned, her smile melted my fear. I caught Billy's lying face and our eyes met. I could never have bluffed like Billy.

'Adios Amigo,' I mouthed and turned the ignition key.

El Fin